MW01632535

SUNSHINE'S SEAL (SPECIAL FORCES: OPERATION ALPHA)

FINDING HOME SERIES, BOOK 4

JULIA BRIGHT

This book is a work of fiction. Names, characters, places, and incidents are products of the author's imagination or used fictitiously. Any resemblance to actual events or locales or persons living or dead is entirely coincidental.

Dear Readers,

Welcome to the Special Forces: Operation Alpha Fan-Fiction world!

If you are new to this amazing world, in a nutshell the author wrote a story using one or more of my characters in it. Sometimes that character has a major role in the story, and other times they are only mentioned briefly. This is perfectly legal and allowable because they are going through Aces Press to publish the story.

This book is entirely the work of the author who wrote it. While I might have assisted with brainstorming and other ideas about which of my characters to use, I didn't have any part in the process or writing or editing the story.

I'm proud and excited that so many authors loved my characters enough that they wanted to write them into their own story. Thank you for supporting them, and me!

READ ON!

Xoxo

Susan Stoker

CHAPTER 1

Sunshine Stephenson shoved her purse into her locker and checked the mirror, making sure her hair wasn't too wild. She tried to tame it before work, but with the humidity on the islands, her hair was a lost cause most days.

"Sun, room three. He needs his vitals," Ricky said as he stepped past her.

She shrugged at her reflection, giving up on her hair. "Another day starts." She clocked in and grabbed the rolling cart with the blood pressure machine. She loved her job and loved living here in Hawaii. But nagging worry ate at her, leaving her sleepless too many nights to count. Sepher, her brother, was out of jail, which wasn't good. At least she no longer lived in California where it would be easy for him to find her. Sepher would have to work to track her down. When she'd run, she hadn't left too many clues and she'd gone far enough away he wouldn't just stumble on her.

Sunshine opened the door for the patient room and met the man's gaze. Soulful brown eyes stared back at her. The man was built with muscles for days. A thick beard covered the lower part of his face, making him look rugged, but kindness exuded from him.

But it was his eyes that were bright and seemed to look into her soul that did her in. She had to swallow hard to keep from gasping.

"I'm Sun, and what's your name?" She stared at his chart, unable to meet his gaze without her tongue hanging out and drooling all over him.

"Ethan Olsen."

"Good, that's a match." She glanced up, trying to be professional, but then her gaze locked with his, and a shiver skated through her. Looking into his eyes was like gazing into desire. She had to stop this. A man like him wouldn't be interested in her. Besides, this man was a patient, not a guy from a dating app on her phone.

She almost rolled her eyes. Two months ago, she'd gotten brave—foolish—and used one of those sites. Never again. The men she attracted only wanted sex, and they lied about it. Heck, they lied about everything. One of the guys who matched with her was married. It sucked that she went out with three different guys from the app, and by the time they were done with the first drink, all three were trying to get into her pants.

She pushed away thoughts of those guys and focused on the man in front of her. "I just need to get your vitals. I'm Dr. Bennet's nurse. Do you have any new concerns?"

"You aren't the same nurse from before."

His gruff voice vibrated through her, making her heart rate speed up. She had to force herself to concentrate on her tasks of getting him checked in, or she'd be lost in his gaze.

"Oops, looks like you need the larger cuff." She couldn't believe she'd started with the tiny blood pressure cuff usually used on small women or large kids. She knew better than to do that with the guys in the military who had muscles for days.

She'd taken the job as a traveling nurse and been thankful to be assigned so quickly to Hawaii. She'd thought positions in Hawaii would go fast, but it was far from the mainland, and visiting family would be difficult for those with family ties.

Thank goodness she never wanted to see her family again.

"Looks good. It's one ten over sixty-two." If she didn't look at his face, she could concentrate. She needed to get his pulse. Her fingers slid over his wrist, and she made the mistake of looking into his eyes. Immediately, she was lost in his gaze. The urge to lean in and kiss him hit. A crash from something dropping in the hall made her jump. She tore her gaze away from his and tried to find his pulse again.

"Your hands are soft."

His words heated her up, and she couldn't concentrate enough to find his pulse. She cleared her throat and forced concentration.

"Pulse isn't too bad either. It's seventy-four."

"How long have you been working here?"

Heat shot up her neck. His question flustered her. She was acting like a fool. "About a month."

"That explains it. I haven't been in over the last month."

She cleared her throat, trying to force a professional front though she wanted to melt into a puddle at his feet. "And how do you feel? Any concerns?" She met his gaze again and had to force herself not to get lost in his deep brown eyes.

"I feel good. No problems."

"That's good. I'll tell the doctor you're ready."

Ethan chuckled, and she turned to look at him, lifting her eyebrows.

"Is there something else?" She wished the something else was her, but she knew it wasn't. Guys didn't throw themselves at her unless it was for sex. Sure, they'd have sex and leave, but they didn't want her. Just certain body parts they could get off on.

"Doctors always take their own time. You can tell him I'm ready, but he won't be here for a while."

Her lips curled up, and she almost reached out to tap his arm. She wanted to be friends with this man. But she would probably never see him again unless they had friends in common.

Who was she kidding? This guy most likely had women crawling all over him. He didn't need to search for dates. A guy like him could just snap his fingers, and women would drop their pants.

"That's usually true. Hopefully, he'll be in to see you before your next birthday."

Ethan threw back his head and laughed. Sunshine took one last look before she headed out to the main hall. As she replaced the chart on the wall, she closed her eyes and tried to commit him to memory.

"Sunshine, is everything okay?" Dr. Bennet asked behind her.

She jumped then spun, wishing he hadn't caught her crushing over some guy. "Yes, sir. Just heading over to the next patient."

Dr. Bennet gave her a sharp nod before grabbing the chart and heading into Ethan's room. She wished she could be in there just to stare into his eyes again.

Why was she obsessing over this guy? He didn't know her, and if he did, he probably wouldn't want anything to do with her. Her life was too messed up for a guy like Ethan Olsen.

Sunshine moved on to her next patient but couldn't push the man from her mind. She knew he was military, but that didn't mean she could go where those guys hung out and try to meet him. Real life didn't work that way. It would be easier for her to catch a shark at a hotel pool than to try to find that guy at one of the island's bars.

She came out of the patient's room and turned to head back to the nurses' station when the exceedingly good-looking Ethan stepped from the exam room. His gaze connected with hers, and she almost sighed. She had to be more professional. No one wanted her hitting on them.

She forced her eyes back to her work, making

sure everything was in the chart correctly for their new patient.

She turned and slammed right into a wall of muscles. Her gaze slid up his chest as her breath came faster. Her cheeks heated, and her body went hot as his hand grasped her arm to steady her. His lips quirked up on one side, and then he winked as he let go of her. He had her number and knew she was into him. She needed a fan or something to cool off.

"I didn't mean to scare you. I was wondering if you'd like to get coffee this Saturday."

His words made no sense. "With me?"

His chuckle rumbled through her, and she had to squeeze her legs together to keep from falling at his feet.

"Yes, I'd like to go get coffee, or tea. It doesn't have to be coffee. Are you free on Saturday?"

She blinked at him, thinking she must have heard him wrong. "You want to get coffee with me?"

He sobered and bent a little, so they were eye to eye. "Just coffee. No pressure. I'd like to get to know you."

Sunshine couldn't wrap her brain around the idea that this exceedingly good-looking man would want to spend time with her. "Um, I'm off on Saturday. So, I guess."

He lifted his eyebrows, and his lips ticked up in a smile. "You guess?"

She waved her hand at him and shook her head. "You're all—well, you. And I'm me."

A line developed between his eyebrows as the skin around his eyes crinkled a little. "I don't know what that means."

"It means she has no confidence," Ricky quipped as he sailed past.

Heat washed over Sunshine. Ricky was right, but she didn't want Ethan to know. His lips curved up more, and he bent, so his mouth was beside her ear.

"I want to see you. I'll meet you on Saturday at Cup of Joe at nine. Is that good?"

She nodded, unable to find her voice. Ethan winked, then turned and strutted out. Maybe he didn't strut, but she did watch him the whole way until the door shut and she couldn't see his perfect behind.

Making it through the rest of the morning was like fighting fog. She didn't make any mistakes, but she had to force concentration. They usually grabbed lunch as they went, not getting a real break, but today she had enough time to sit down and eat her sandwich. Ricky stepped into the kitchen and whistled.

"Girl, that guy is H O T hot."

Heat filled her face. "I have no clue why he asked me out. I shouldn't go."

"Oh honey, you'd better go, or I'm stealing your food for the next month. You don't leave a man like that hanging."

"Don't touch my food," Sunshine snarked as she wrapped one arm in front of her food to keep Ricky away.

Laughter filled the room as he grabbed his bag from the refrigerator and popped a container into the microwave. "Then you'd better go out with that guy. He's sexy."

Sunshine rolled her eyes. "I don't care about that. I just want a guy to treat me like a human and not a sex doll."

"Well, he could—"

"Don't say it," Sunshine said before he had a chance to finish his sentence. The phone buzzed, and Sunshine answered. Their receptionist took a lunch break, so one of them had the phone from noon to one. She dealt with the call, scheduling the person for later that afternoon.

"Looks like we're going to be busy," Ricky said.

"Aren't we always?"

She liked keeping busy, though. It beat sitting around just waiting for someone to show up. When she worked in Louisiana for a few months, it had been so boring. She was glad they were kept busy here in this office. It wasn't so bad that she had to stay until six each evening, either. She didn't work weekends, and she was home in time to unwind. This was so much better than the high-pressured ER rotations she'd worked for a few years and much better than doing nothing. She liked the doctor, and she enjoyed the area. Maybe she would stay for a while.

Thoughts of Ethan filled her mind, and she wondered if he was too good to be true. The good-looking guys never wanted her. She wasn't a blonde-haired beauty. Instead, her Pacific Island and Native American roots mixed with the other races that made up her family and left her looking plain in her own eyes. Her grandmother was part Chinese and had married a guy whose grandfather was black and his mother, Irish. If they had a family reunion, it would look more like a gathering of nations instead of just one family. As far back as anyone talked about, no one in her direct family line had married anyone of the same race. Even her great, great, great grandmother from Japan had gone against her parents' wishes and married a Spanish sailor. She thought she looked too plain and too different from most American girls. Back in high school, people called her a mutt. It didn't help that Sepher was a jerk who liked to abuse her.

Maybe this Ethan guy would realize she wasn't worth the trouble and wouldn't even show up. She'd had plenty of dates like that over the years. She shouldn't even go, but then Ricky would find out, and he'd be hell to deal with. There wasn't an easy way out. She would deal with the humiliation and find some convenient lie to tell Ricky about how the guy didn't show or something. It would be better than revealing how he'd met with her and then decided she wasn't worth his time, just like the majority of men found her not worth theirs.

CHAPTER 2

Ethan "Minx" Olsen ducked low, then rolled, pulling his rifle into position before taking two shots, delivering one to the head and one to the heart of the dummy they were shooting at.

"Good job, Minx," Vine called out.

He stood and stretched, glad the doctor had given him the all-clear. He hated that he'd been sidelined because of some stupid illness. Maybe he should have been taking better care of his body, but he hadn't done anything really wrong. He'd taken a few too many painkillers, and then, boom, the ulcer started eating away at him. At least he'd gotten the problem solved and could get back to work.

"We've missed you," Astro said as he stepped

close and delivered a clap on Minx's shoulder. "You are one of a kind."

"Jesus, don't get all emotional on me," Minx said.

"Awww, but we love you," Legs said.

"Stop being so sappy." Minx missed these guys, too. Missed the way they joked around. It had been hell being sidelined, and he never wanted to experience that again. From now on, he was going to take care of his body.

"Hey, we're thinking about going surfing in the morning," Vine called out as they collected their gear.

"I have something," Minx said as he thought of the cute nurse he planned to meet at the coffee shop close to the hospital. He should have picked a better place, but it was honestly the first place he'd thought of when he'd asked her out.

Worry filled Wig's face. "Wait, what are you doing? It's not health-related, right?"

Minx rolled his eyes. "No."

"What are you doing tomorrow that you can't come with us?" Quirk asked.

Minx didn't know why he didn't want to tell them about his possible date with Sun, the beautiful nurse he'd met the other day. Maybe because she hadn't seemed enthusiastic to go out with him. "I'm just doing something."

"Oh shit, Minx has a date," Wig said.

"Nice. Who are you going out with?" Astro asked.

"Jesus. It may or may not be a date." The guys were incredibly intrusive. They'd keep asking questions no matter what he said or did. They weren't the type to ever give up. He knew they would stay on him until he spilled his guts.

"Where did you meet her?" Quirk asked.

He huffed out a breath and told them about meeting Sun at the doctor's appointment. They razzed him, like usual, but when he headed out for the evening, they all wished him well on the date. His stomach twisted and turned that evening, and he ended up needing to work out to wear himself out before dropping into bed. He woke with the sun and hopped out of his bed, ready for the day to start. He still had two hours before meeting Sun, so he did another workout to keep himself from climbing the walls.

When he arrived at the coffee shop, he ordered a bagel with an egg and sausage. He hoped she wasn't a vegan, or if she was, she didn't mind him eating meat.

Since he'd arrived early he finished most of his

sandwich when the door opened and Sun stepped in. He glanced up and froze as she flipped her glorious hair behind her shoulder. The sun streamed in, highlighting her form. The skirt she wore was thin, and her shirt did little to hide her natural assets with the sun blazing behind her.

He was glad he wasn't chewing food or drinking at that moment because he surely would have choked. She looked like a dream. He doubted she understood exactly how thin her skirt was. But man, oh man, he was glad she was here to see him.

Minx stood and took two steps, closing the distance between them. "Good morning." He sounded like he'd run a mile instead of just taking two steps. She'd taken his breath away, leaving him panting. He really had it bad for her.

Her nose wrinkled as she stared up at him. "Hi. I was so nervous I almost chickened out."

A flash of panic lit through him. "Why were you nervous?"

She swallowed, and he vowed right then to make sure she knew he really was interested. He noticed her hands shaking, so he took one of them, which seemed small in his oversized hand.

"Let me get you coffee, or do you like tea?"

"I'd best go with tea. I've been up for a while and drank too much coffee already."

He led her to the order counter, and she ordered a tea and no food. His gaze narrowed as he watched her open her purse.

"How about a sandwich or a bagel?"

Sun shook her head and glanced up, worry clouding her eyes. "No. I'm good."

He doubted she was, but he wasn't going to push her on this. He had cash out and handed it to the woman at the counter, not giving Sun a chance to pay.

Her gaze shot to his, her eyes went wide and her mouth fell open. "You didn't—"

"Of course I did. I invited you here. I'm paying."

Her eyes narrowed, and then she rolled them before she grabbed her tea. They sat at the table where he'd been earlier. Her gaze flitted to him, then away so often he thought she might get dizzy. He wanted to tell her to chill, but he doubted she would listen.

"How long have you been in Hawaii?" He figured that was an easy question.

"Um, not long. I moved here for a traveling nurse position."

“How does that work? The traveling nurse thing?”

“There are areas that have shortages, and they don’t necessarily want to hire a full-time nurse. This position opened up, and I think I was the first person to apply. I was lucky to get it.”

“Did you live in Hawaii before?”

Sun’s gaze flicked away before she shook her head. “No. I do like the islands, though. I hope I can find another post when this one is finished.”

A sliver of panic lodged in his chest. He didn’t want her to leave. “How long will you be here?”

“I’m signed on for fifty weeks. So another forty-five weeks at least.”

He breathed a sigh of relief. He wanted her to be here as long as he was, but they could talk about that later. He didn’t want to scare her off by being way too clingy. They didn’t know each other, and they might not be a good fit. She could turn out to be totally different from how he saw her.

She took another sip of her tea, and he took a bite of his food. He liked watching her. When the door opened, she jumped, then turned to look at who was coming in. He didn’t know what the weird look on her face was about, but it made the hair on his neck stand on end. Who was she looking out for?

The urge to question her, drilling in and getting information washed over him. She probably would freak out if he did that. He needed to spend more time with her before he started asking her intrusive questions.

"Would you like to go for a walk? There is a park about a block away. The weather isn't too hot yet."

Sun nodded. "That would be nice."

He finished his sandwich, and they stepped outside. The sun had risen a little more since he'd stepped into the coffee shop, and the day was heating up. It wouldn't be terrible, but if they stayed in the sun too long, it would be warm.

Walking beside Sun, he couldn't help but glance at her, taking in her high cheekbones, her lush lips, her honey-colored eyes, the way her nose sloped, and the curve of her neck. Desire whipped through him and he wanted to kiss her. She wasn't his and might not ever be, but he wanted to be the one to hold her close and so much more.

"You're staring at me," Sun said.

"It's because you're beautiful."

Sun burst out laughing, and Minx frowned at her. Her eyebrows raised as she stared at him.

She shook her head as her eyes narrowed. "I'm really not."

He took her hand, lifted it to his mouth, and then brushed his lips over her knuckles. "You really are very beautiful. The moment I saw you, I knew I wanted to know more about you."

She looked down and stared at the ground. He moved, so he was blocking her path. She jerked her head up, her eyes on his as her expression turned serious.

"I'm not that good-looking."

He cupped her cheek and leaned in, brushing his lips over her forehead. "But you are. You're incredibly good-looking. I think you're the best-looking woman I've seen."

Her eyes narrowed. "I question your ability to understand the truth."

He saw her lack of confidence as a challenge. He'd dated women who knew exactly how pretty they were, which tended to make them uglier with each passing day. He would enjoy being with Sun.

He moved to the side so they could keep walking. "Do you like being a nurse?"

Sun shrugged. "It's good. There are times I question my career choice."

"Like when?"

"I worked in a facility in Alabama for a few months. It was terrible. The place I worked in

Louisianan was better but boring. I like working here."

"Where did you grow up?"

Sun swallowed and glanced away. Her eyes narrowed, and her nose wrinkled. "I don't like talking about that time."

A warning went off at the back of his mind. He needed to figure out what that was about. They walked for more than a minute and she seemed more closed off after that question.

"Do you like chocolate or vanilla ice cream?" he asked to throw her off. Had she been upset thinking about her past? Maybe ice cream was a neutral enough subject to get her to enjoy their time together.

Laughter bubbled up, and she shook her head. "Why would I limit myself? I love rum raisin and butter pecan. I also like pistachio. Then there are the complex flavors that don't have any rhyme or reason. Some of my favorites are buttered baguette with peach sauce or toasted coconut with chocolate chips."

"Obviously, you are an ice cream connoisseur. I think you should take me out to discover unique ice cream flavors."

The skin around Sun's eyes crinkled as she

smiled. "You do?"

Minx tried to stay serious as he nodded. "I think it's a matter of national security."

Her laughter bubbled up and tinkled along his nerves. His cock tightened at the sound, and he had to think of something awful to get it to go down. He didn't want her thinking he just wanted sex. He wanted sex, but he also wanted late nights laughing about nothing, warm mornings working in the yard, holidays with too much food, and movies they watched just holding hands. He wanted the magic that comes with finding someone special. If they dropped their drawers and had sex right now, the magic would be frightened away. He needed long-term from this woman, not a few hours of sweaty grinding.

"That look in your eyes," Sun said.

"What look?" He tried to appear innocent, like he'd not been making plans for them for next year, and the year after and twenty years from now.

Sun narrowed her gaze as she studied him. "What are you thinking?"

"That we should go wander around the Bishop Museum then find somewhere to eat lunch."

Sun eyebrows rose. "You want to spend time with me?"

He resisted the urge to pull her into a crushing kiss and show her how he felt about spending time with her. He settled for nodding as he spoke. "Yeah, I really do."

"But I'm—"

He placed his fingers on her lips, stopping her doubting words. "It would be an honor to spend the day getting to know you. We can worry about other things later. Right now, I just want to find out more about you."

Her nose crinkled. "Are you sure?"

"Very sure."

He couldn't think of anything he'd rather do than spend the day with Sun, getting to know her. To him, it felt like a connection existed between them. He wanted to explore that connection and see how far it developed. If he was right about his hunch, they would have what he felt would be deep enough to give them a lasting relationship. Sun just had to agree to see him.

CHAPTER 3

At some point, she wanted to start living her life again. Could she, though? The threat of Sepher finding her and then doing something unimaginable hung over her head. The last time he'd found her, the two women in the apartment below her ended up dead. She'd escaped, but at what cost? Those two women had been her friends. They certainly hadn't known what Sepher would do. She'd heard about the murders in California after she'd taken off. Since then, she'd tried not to get too close to anyone.

Right now, she was flying under the radar. She didn't have any social media, nothing under her name. Her phone was a burner phone, her email random. Sure, her work was under her name, but because she'd hired on with the travel nursing program, she wasn't listed on doctors' websites. The program also wouldn't give out her name or location, even to family members. If Sepher tried to search for her through her employer, he'd be given the option of sending a message through the service. He'd have no way to contact her directly.

"This museum isn't your style, is it?" Ethan asked.

Sunshine shook her head. "It isn't that. It's..." Her words hung in the air long enough for Ethan to develop lines between his eyebrows.

"What?" Ethan placed a hand on her arm, giving her warmth. "You can tell me anything."

Could she? She wanted to believe his words, but she needed to play it safe. Eventually, she would tell him, but she needed to keep the weirdness of her family hidden for a little while longer.

"I'm just a little surprised you wanted to spend the day with me. I like this museum. My great grandfather was Hawaiian."

Ethan's eyebrows shot up. "Really?"

"Yes. I have a lot of different races and cultures in my background. No one was satisfied sticking with what they knew. I have a lot of relatives who were kicked out of their families because they married a different race."

"Wow, that sounds interesting. I'd like to know more."

They wandered into another room that was full of artifacts. "I like this room. It feels good in here."

"I'd like to see you tomorrow," Ethan said.

Sunshine paused. He wanted a second date. She glanced up into his eyes, wondering how she'd gotten a guy to look at her with such devotion.

"You do know this is as good as it gets. Like I don't turn into a princess when the clock strikes midnight."

Ethan leaned in and brushed his lips against hers. He didn't move away when the kiss ended. Instead, he stayed close, so they were eye to eye. "I don't want you to change at all. I like this." He picked up a strand of her hair, then ran his hand over her shoulder. "And this. I like you."

She shook her head, wondering why this beautiful man had chosen to be with her. Guys didn't want her. She'd seen it time and time again in Alabama, Louisiana, and of course, when she was younger, in California. She wasn't prime dating material. And then, if she did find someone, her brother showed up and ruined it all.

"Let's get out of here." Ethan led her to the exit and to his SUV. They were silent on the drive to the beach. He parked, then hopped out, moving around the back of the vehicle to her side to help her out. There weren't many people on the beach, just a few scattered here and there.

Sun slipped off her shoes and let out a sigh of relief when her feet hit the sand. The sand between her toes felt good.

They'd gone about fifty feet when Ethan spoke. "I don't know who hurt you, and I don't know where you got the idea that you aren't desirable, but I can assure you with certainty, you are very desirable. And I'm not going to hurt you."

Sun didn't know what to say. A shiver skated through her, shaking her all the way to her knees. His words twisted through her mind, making her wonder if he was for real.

She lifted her hand and touched his beard, then the skin of his cheek. She ran her fingers up to his forehead, then down to his neck.

She squinted up at him, probably not a sexy look, but she wasn't trying for sexy. Instead, she was trying to understand. "You're not some figment of my imagination. You're real."

His laughter barked out, making her jump and pull her hand back. He reached out and took her hand, weaving their fingers together. The way their fingers naturally intertwined felt right. Like they belonged together. Another shiver snaked through her. She wanted this too much. It was too good to be true.

"Yes, I'm very much real." He tucked her hand into the crook of his elbow and continued walking. "So tomorrow, I'd like you to meet some of my friends."

"Really?"

"Yes. I want you to see that we're a good group of people. I'm not going anywhere." He stopped walking, and his expression grew serious. "Well, I do have to leave at a moment's notice sometimes."

She shook her head and narrowed her eyes. "Wait, what? You are, or you aren't going anywhere?"

"I'm military. I know that was obvious at the doctor's office. I'm on a special team, and we don't just deploy on a timed schedule. Though I have those types of deployments. Mine is about eighteen months away. But there are times when things happen, and my team is needed. We sometimes get notice and other times we're woken up in the middle of the night and told to be on base in an hour or less."

"Oh." She had no idea if he was being truthful or pulling her leg.

"This is why I want you to meet the rest of the gang."

"So they can corroborate your story?"

"No and yes. I'd like you to maybe get one of the women's phone numbers, so if we have to dash out of town you aren't just left thinking I abandoned you. There are times we're gone for weeks, and people left at home have no clue where we are."

"That sounds odd—no, dangerous."

His lips quirked up, and she smiled up at him, lost in the kindness in his deep brown eyes. His breath hitched, and he lowered, holding his lips next to hers for a moment. She closed the distance, sensing he was waiting for her to move.

His tongue pushed at her lips, begging her to open. She didn't hold back and plastered her body against his as she opened for him. His arms that had held her loosely before wrapped around her so one hand was reaching around to the side of her breast, and the other hand was on her ass, holding her close.

She moaned as her pelvis brushed against the hard ridge in his pants. There was no hiding how he felt about her. She should pull back and take this slowly, but desire flashed through her, and she gave in to her needs, clinging to this big bear of a man.

When the kiss ended, and he set her back on the

sidewalk—she hadn't realized he'd been holding her up—he wiped his big hand over his face and shook his head.

"You stoke every fire in my veins. If we were alone, I'd pull your clothes off and take you to my bed."

His words heated her, leaving her wanting him so hard she leaned in, pressing her hand against his chest. He took her hand and kissed each finger, his gaze never leaving hers.

"Tell me more about yourself, your childhood, your family."

His words were cold water splashed in her face. She took a step back as reality hit. She couldn't get tangled up with this man. He would be at risk. Sepher would attack and leave him for dead. The one guy she'd cared about was six feet under, his life taken by Sepher.

"What's wrong?" Ethan asked.

She shook her head and held up her hand, backing away. "Nothing. I just—"

"Hey," Ethan's strong voice made her pause and glance up.

Everything stalled in her mind as he stepped close, his expression sharp as a knife. Another shiver worked through her as the desire to lean in grew. Desire took over as she stared into his eyes.

"Tell me exactly what happened with your family." His words were stiff, unbending. The command in his voice pulled at her, and she wanted to obey. But the fear deep inside made her hesitate.

"Why do you think something happened with my family?"

His eyebrows furrowed so hard she almost gasped. His hand came up and caressed her cheek. He was hard and unbending but sweet and gentle.

"Sweet Sun, tell me everything so I can help you."

She wanted to believe he could. "But he's evil."

"Darling, I eat evil for breakfast and shit it out by noon. He won't stand up against me."

She turned to pace away, then spun back, fear and pain slicing at her so hard she didn't know if she could survive the next onslaught from her family if it came, but knowing if she was beside this man, he would save her. Could she put him through that? He didn't deserve the pain that would come when her family attacked.

"I'm afraid."

His expression changed in a flash as he moved beside her, taking her in his arms, holding her like she was the most precious person in the world. "I'm here."

She shook her head against his chest. "That shouldn't make me feel better, but it does."

"Tell me what happened?"

She blew out a breath and closed her eyes. "I don't want you to die."

She clung to him, knowing she had to let him go. There wasn't any way she would survive if Sepher came looking for her and killed this wonderful man. Her life was too screwed up to stay with Ethan, though she wanted nothing more than to spend her life in this man's arms.

CHAPTER 4

Minx's stomach dropped at her words, and he had to draw in a slow breath. He didn't want to die either, but he didn't think she was talking about him being safe on missions.

Her family was messed up, that much was obvious based on her reactions. He just didn't know how screwed up they were, and that was exactly what he needed to find out.

"Sun—"

"It's actually Sunshine. I just shorten it when I'm at work."

"Sunshine. I like that."

"My parents were weird. I took heat when I was a kid being called Sunshine. It sucked, and we moved around a lot, so every single new school I got it over and over again."

"Kids can be cruel."

"Very."

"So tell me what your family did to you that has you so scared."

Sunshine stepped away and wrapped her arms around her waist. "My brother's name is Sepher Dickens. His dad is different from mine, so his last name isn't Stephenson like mine."

She shivered, and Minx moved to her, not touching but standing close. She looked up, and pain shone in her eyes. He wanted to pull her close, but he felt she needed to talk without interruption.

"He had an unnatural attraction to me."

Her meaning came through loud and clear. Minx's muscles tightened as anger whipped through him. He squeezed his hands into fists, tamping down the anger inside. He would kill Sepher if the man ever came looking for Sunshine.

"I was seventeen and dating this guy, Michael. I might have been in love with him. It's so different when you're a teenager. I told myself I loved him, but, anyway, I liked him and he liked me. We pledged to be together forever like only teenagers can promise. Sepher came over and found Michael and me kissing. That weekend Michael ended up dying. The cops never figured out who killed him, but I knew."

Minx had to fight the urge to interrupt her and pull her close, promising to keep her safe. He didn't know Sepher, and he couldn't say he could best him in any fight, but he was fairly sure he could make a good effort of destroying the jerk.

"Sepher grabbed me a few nights later and took me back to his house. He held me in his basement. I escaped about four weeks later and took off. I lived in California for a few years, getting a nursing degree. I was happy and thought I was free, but he found me. I ran to Mississippi but didn't stay long. That's when I found out about the traveling nursing program and took a position in Alabama, then Louisiana. When Hawaii opened up, I was thrilled."

She turned to face him, and he spied a single tear running down her cheek. He swiped it away and pulled her to him, so her head was resting against his chest. He prayed his heartbeat calmed her, giving her strength. But she stiffened and stepped back.

"That's why I can't get involved. I may have to run."

He cupped her cheeks and lowered to brush a

kiss over her mouth. “Sunshine, your days of running are over. I’ll be here to keep you safe.”

“I don’t want him to kill you.”

“Babe, I’m a trained killer. That’s what I do in the military. He may try to come after you, but he won’t succeed.”

“I don’t want you to have to do something like that. If you kill him and get caught, you could end up in jail.”

“I’ll make sure it looks bad for him and good for us. His days of harming you are over.”

Sunshine stared up at him like he was her savior, and maybe he was. He sure as hell wasn’t going to allow some idiot to keep taking advantage of her. She deserved happiness and a life.

“You can’t promise me that. Michael promised nothing would happen.”

He shook his head. “You’re right, but I’ll be by your side, hopefully making you happy for years. If he comes after you, I’ll fight to keep him away. Live and be happy today. None of us, and I do mean none of us are ever guaranteed tomorrow. Let me make your todays good. Give me a chance to be the person you need me to be, and we can be happy together.”

She shook her head which sent panic through

him. "Do I deserve any happiness? Michael is dead because of me."

"No, he's dead because of Sepher. You didn't kill Michael."

"I'd never forgive myself if something happened to you."

He cupped her cheek and pulled her in for a kiss. Her lips lingered against his, and he took the kiss deep, pulling her so close he could feel every curve of her body. Desire pumped hot and heavy through him. He wanted to wrap her legs around his waist and take her right there. He wouldn't, not in public.

When she stepped back, he took the chance and asked. "Come back to my place?"

She glanced out at the ocean then back to him. "Will you dump me right after we have sex?"

"Not a chance. We don't even have to have sex. I just want to spend more time with you."

"If I say no?"

"Then tomorrow I'll pick you up, and we'll go meet my friends. If you don't want to spend the night, I'm okay with that. I just like spending time with you. I like being with you."

She lifted her hand then hesitated for a moment before cupping his cheek. "I want to say yes, but I'm afraid."

"I understand. I do. How about I make sure you get home, then tomorrow I'll pick you up and we can spend time together? You'll see I'm not going to run off."

"Okay."

He wouldn't lie, he wanted to fuck her brains out, but he wouldn't push the issue. He could go home and jerk himself off. He wanted Sunshine, but he wanted her for a long time. Just having sex today wouldn't be enough. They belonged together, he just had to find a way for them to make this work.

CHAPTER 5

Sunshine couldn't believe the tribe of people Ethan had collected were for real. This seemed like some made-up fairytale. Then again, she'd never known anyone really in the military. Sure, the hospital where she worked now was military, but most of the people she worked with were civilians, and she'd never gotten close to a patient until Ethan.

"So you're telling me you all help each other. Like Ethan wasn't lying to me when he told me how you all support each other?" Sunshine was speaking to a woman named Jenna, who seemed too good to be true.

Jenna's laughter spilled over the area. "Yes. I get that few people really are like this, but our men do a lot."

Sunshine turned to look at the group of men who were talking about something in low tones as they cooked the burgers on the grill. They were at a park next to the beach that wasn't too packed. Occasionally commercial planes flew past. The guys ignored those, but they all turned and watched when military planes flew by.

"They do?" Sunshine asked.

"Yes. You do know what type of job he has in the Navy?" Jenna asked.

She shook her head. "No. I didn't even know he was in the Navy."

"He's a SEAL. You know what they are?"

Sunshine shrugged. "Not really. I mean, I know there were a few movies about them, but I don't know anything more."

"Well, they really are badasses," Jenna said.

"Who's a badass?" Becky asked as she came close. She and Ashley had walked over to the restrooms about twenty feet away and were back now. Ashley had a bump that looked like a baby bump, but Sunshine wouldn't ask unless they brought it up.

"The guys," Jenna said.

"They really are," Ashley said. "Before they rescued me, I really thought it was the end."

"Wait, what?" Sunshine glanced around the

group, unsure if she should believe them about the rescue. "They rescued you?"

All three women chuckled. "We all met our men when they were dispatched to rescue the group we were with," Jenna said.

Becky lifted her drink and raised her shoulder in a shrug. "I was held by human traffickers. I'm still in therapy. Then my ex abducted me when I arrived in Dallas. He held me prisoner in his house for a month. If Astro hadn't come to save me, I would be dead."

Sunshine may have gasped. "God, that's awful."

"I was a part of a government organization and working for a senator at the time. He was dealing with a terrorist. The team came in and saved us. Then the senator came back and had me abducted to be sold off in Mexico."

"Shit," Sunshine said as she stared at the women.

"I'm an oceanographer. I was mapping the ocean floor and some World War Two ships that sank in the Indian Ocean when one of the scrappers attacked. They took me to a brothel. It was awful."

"Jesus. And I thought I had it bad."

Jenna lifted her eyebrows. "Hey, just because we had shit happen to us doesn't mean your shit isn't bad. What happened to you?"

Sunshine glanced around and then rolled her eyes. "Sorry, I don't usually share this, and it's hard to talk about."

"We know people judge you based on what happens in your life," Ashley said.

"And honestly, we don't tell everyone we meet what happened," Becky said.

Jenna placed her hand on Sunshine's arm. "It's just because Minx called and told us all that you were special. He wants you to know we're not fair-weather friends. We're here for you."

Sunshine blew out a breath and shook her head. "I've never had that before."

"Well, now you do. Tell us what happened," Ashley said as she took a seat, groaning as she lowered.

Both Becky and Jenna moved to hold her hand. Sunshine narrowed her gaze and really looked at Ashley.

"Are you due soon?" Sunshine slapped her hand over her mouth. "I'm sorry. That's none of my business."

"It's okay. I have a few weeks still. I took a new Pilates class yesterday, and it's killing me. It's supposed to help with delivery, but right now, I'm not feeling it."

"It's my fault," Jenna said. "I'm pregnant, too, but not as far along as Ashley. I talked her into taking the class. I should have kept my mouth closed."

Ashley shook her head. "No, I need it. My legs aren't anywhere near as toned as they need to be. Labor will be hard. I want anything that makes it easier."

"Congratulations," Sunshine said.

"Thank you. I wasn't expecting to get pregnant so soon after meeting Robert. We were using protection, but I guess things happen."

Sunshine nodded. "They do."

"So tell us about you. We want to be here to help if we can," Jenna said.

Sunshine spilled everything, even the part about her brother raping her, her getting pregnant when she was thirteen, and then losing the baby.

"Oh God, that's awful." Becky jumped up and pulled her into a hug. "I'm so sorry that happened to you. Every part of that is terrible. I know you weren't ready for a baby at that age but losing it must have done a number on you."

Sunshine shrugged, her stomach twisting from Becky being so nice. "I felt bad about losing it, like I did something terribly wrong. I was young and wanted that baby—or thought I did. Of course, now that I'm older and understand what my brother did to me, I'm glad I don't have a child out there somewhere because there's no way I would have been able to keep it."

Jenna hugged her next. "I'm so sorry."

Ashley's belly poked her when they hugged, and a tear escaped her eyes, then another.

"Why are you all making Sunshine cry?" Ethan asked.

Horror filled Sunshine. She didn't want to tell Ethan about this. Jenna pulled her close and whispered to her.

"You need to tell him. He needs to know. Trust me, he won't judge you."

A shiver snaked through Sunshine's body, and more tears fell. Ethan groaned and pulled her away from Jenna, holding her close.

"She needs you," Ashley said as she walked away.

Suddenly they were alone. Everyone else had gone off to the other side of the grill. The women were right, she needed to tell Ethan everything, but she didn't want him to leave her over this. She didn't know if she could have kids or not. Because of Sepher, she'd never thought she'd have a chance at a future. And what man would want her anyway?

"What's up, babe? What can I help you with?"

She shook her head as more tears escaped. "I'm so ashamed."

"You don't have anything to be ashamed about."

She swiped at her eyes and blew her nose on the napkin Ethan handed her. "I didn't tell you everything."

"I'm here." Ethan sat at the picnic table, facing away from the guys. He pulled her onto his lap and held on to her. "Tell me."

Another sob wracked her body. "M-my brother had more than just an unhealthy attraction to me. I was thirteen and pregnant with his child."

Ethan stiffened underneath her, and she was sure this was it. He was going to dump her. She closed her eyes and continued. Might as well tell him everything, then he could walk away knowing he'd dodged a bullet.

"I lost the baby, so there isn't a child out there I've given birth to. I'm sorry."

His breath left his body in a rush. "Oh God, you have nothing to be sorry for."

"I don't know if I can carry a baby."

"I don't care about that. I care about you. I want you. If we never have children, then we never have them. I care that you were hurt so badly as a child."

"I was a teenager."

"Thirteen is still a child. I was an idiot at thirteen, and my biggest worry was *Minecraft* and *Skyrim*. I didn't have sex until I was almost eighteen. It didn't even enter my mind. I mean, I jerked off, but that was all me. No one forced anything on me and no one touched me."

"I didn't understand back then, and it felt good. I didn't know it was so wrong."

"Babe, how old were you when he started doing that to you?"

She shrugged. "I don't know. I was young, too young to say no. My mom used to leave us alone, and he would crawl into bed with me. I remember being about seven, and he shoved his dick in my mouth."

Ethan held her close, and she swore she heard him crying. She leaned back, and sure enough, there were tears in his eyes.

"Why are you crying?"

"Because I wish I'd known you. I would have killed him to get you away from him."

She had no words. She couldn't believe Ethan cared about her. She hadn't ever told anyone the full story, not about the baby and having to suck her brother's dick before she turned eight. The people she told parts of the story to either dumped her or walked away. She couldn't believe Ethan cared so much to cry for her. They stayed huddled together for a long moment.

Finally, she wiped her eyes and sat up. "I'm good now."

He kissed her cheeks then her forehead. "I'm sure you are. But you still have that in your past, and you're running from your brother now."

"It would take a lot for him to find me."

He caressed her cheek. "I want to keep you safe."

"How?"

"I'm going to contact a guy I know. He'll put a tracer on your brother. Then we'll know if he heads this way. I just want you to be safe."

She closed her eyes as deep emotions filled her. She'd spent her whole life wondering if anyone would ever be on her side. She didn't think it was possible, and now she had a man who wanted to keep her safe. Could this be real?

"I don't think I ever thought I would be free of him. I really thought he would just be a part of my life forever. I can't believe you actually want to help me."

"Babe, I'm the real deal. I'll take care of you. The food is almost done, and my friends care about you. Let's go eat."

Heat rushed up her neck to her face. "Oh God, they're going to know what happened."

"You have nothing to be embarrassed about. You were abused, and my guys won't judge you for that. They'll help me keep you safe. None of their women will judge you either. You've got nothing to worry about with them."

She glanced over at the group then back to Ethan. "Are you sure?"

"Yes, Sunshine. I'm one hundred percent positive you are accepted in our group. They care about you, just like I do."

She shook her head, and he grabbed her chin, so she had to look into his eyes.

"We don't know each other very well, but I promise to always be here for you."

She stared at him, her eyes going wide. "I'm shocked you want me. Especially after everything I told you."

"You are not the abuse you suffered. You are a good person, and I care about you."

"So you aren't sickened by the fact I was pregnant with—"

"Look at me." Ethan held her gaze. "Sunshine, you have done nothing wrong. I care about you. You are not to blame. I don't want you to think badly about yourself or talk badly."

She nodded, then leaned her forehead against his chest. She couldn't believe this man accepted her, that his friends accepted her. It was hard to believe this group of women took her in and wanted to be friends. She wasn't lost and alone anymore. She had someone who cared. Sunshine just prayed her brother didn't find her because if he did, he would ruin everything good.

CHAPTER 6

Minx hung up the phone and let out a string of curses right as Vine stepped inside.

"Whoa, what's up?" Vine set his pack down, then stretched his arms over his head and leaned to the right, then to the left.

"Tex can't find where Sepher is living—that's Sunshine's brother. He'll keep looking, but the guy's location isn't obvious and that worries me."

Vine blew out a breath. "That's rough. I know you haven't told me everything, and Jenna said it wasn't her story to tell, but I get that he's a very bad guy. The type of people we don't mind taking off this earth."

"You could say that." Minx rolled his shoulders, trying to release some of the stress.

"Jenna is looking into some stuff, too. I mean, her accounts are limited, but she has placed a few calls. This upset her. She was so worked up she had to work out to get any sleep these last few nights."

Minx ran his hand over his face. "Man, I'm sorry."

"Don't be. I'm one of the things she works out on."

Vine's quip made him chuckle. Minx was trying hard to be normal around Sunshine. The last thing she needed was him moping about because of what had happened to her. She'd lived through it and recovered, and he could get through this without turning into an asshole.

"Hey, Vine," Mustang said as he stepped into the room.

"Mustang, how's it going?"

"Good. We have a meeting in five minutes. Captain wants Astro to join us."

Vine broke out into a huge smile. "So he's finally going to get his team."

"Shit," Minx said.

"We all know it's coming," Vine said before he grabbed his bag to store it.

Minx and the whole team knew it was coming, which meant they would get a new team member soon. He hoped they weren't broken up too much.

The Navy didn't usually rip apart whole teams and force them to reorganize. At least they recognized the teams were like family. He liked the guys on Mustang's team, but there were some guys he'd met in Coronado who rubbed him the wrong way. It was his job, and he could put up with almost anyone, but these guys were his brothers.

Minx hoped whoever stepped into Astro's shoes wasn't a jerk. He had enough to deal with. He didn't need to be on asshole watch.

Whatever meeting Vine, Mustang, and Astro were in wasn't talked about after, which meant they weren't headed out on a mission. After work, he stopped by the commissary and picked up food for dinner. Sunshine would be at his place at six. That gave him time to get in a quick workout and shower.

He couldn't believe that someone like her wanted him. She had her life together, or it seemed that way to him. Sure, she was hiding from her brother, but she had built a life that wasn't too bad. He knew she'd been through hell as a child, and he just wanted to make her life better.

As a SEAL, he'd seen some nasty shit. He'd lost friends to war, had buddies blown to bits, and transported them back to a ship where they were kept alive long enough to get them to some hospital state-side. Some were still alive though they were missing so much of their body they needed constant care. It was tough seeing guys who didn't have any issues with being at the top of their physical game suddenly not even be able to walk or pick up a chip and eat.

Two of the guys he went through basic with were in that situation now. He'd kept in touch throughout the years, celebrating each other's accomplishments. When he'd graduated BUDs, they'd been his family in the audience. It was hard to see them now. They Facetimed every few weeks. Both of them got dumped, and they were living with their parents, but one of them found a woman who was prepared to be with him. The power of kindness and love amazed him. That was real strength.

Sunshine's injuries weren't visible, but she'd gone through hell like his buddies. She had come out on the other side and was victorious. His buddies had good attitudes still. They weren't wallowing in self-pity. Sure, they had physical issues, but they looked at life as a gift. He wasn't sure he could do it. He would have to stay strong for Sunshine. That meant whatever his buddies had, whether it was grit or determination that kept them going, he would do it. Sunshine deserved as much.

The knock at his door had him going half-hard. Jesus, it was like he was a teenager again. When he opened the door and saw Sunshine, his dick took over, going full-hard. She was it for him. Maybe she wasn't what others would call classically beautiful, but she was the best-looking woman he'd ever seen. She had plenty of curves, too. He wanted someone he could hold on to, and she fit into his arms perfectly.

He shut the door behind her then pulled her into a hug that ended with him up against the wall, her between his legs, their bodies pressed together. He wanted to strip off her clothes, but the timer rang on the food.

"Food's done," Sunshine said before stepping away.

"Jesus." He swiped his hand over his face and watched as his girlfriend practically skipped down the hall.

"You're in a good mood," he said.

"I am. I have tomorrow off, and I get to spend it with the best guy I know."

His lips quirked up. "We haven't put a label on this. You're my girlfriend, right?"

She shrugged. "I don't like labels. But I'm not going to see anyone else. I like you, Ethan."

He took the food from the oven and set it on the stovetop before he turned to face her. "I like you. A lot."

Sunshine came close and walked her fingers up the center of his torso to his neck. He blew out a breath as desire kicked up.

"I don't plan on being with anyone else. So girlfriend fits, but it's not encompassing enough. I feel like we've made a connection."

Minx held her gaze, searching for any subterfuge. He didn't find any. She was his. He saw that much shining in her eyes.

"I don't know how we grew so close so fast, but I have these feelings for you."

"I totally understand what you mean. I have these feelings for you that aren't small."

"I know this is a little fast, but do you think it's time you kept a toothbrush over here? Maybe a change of clothes? And if I gave you a key, would you feel comfortable letting yourself in if I wasn't here?"

Sunshine grabbed a plate and started serving him food before making up her own plate. She hadn't answered, and he thought maybe he'd said too much.

"Are you sure you're ready for me to have a key? I don't want to press the issue. Your place is close to the hospital. Like it took me the same amount of time to get here tonight as it does to get home most days."

"That's good. I like this area. It's quiet, not a lot of traffic."

Sunshine chuckled. "My area is way too busy. I hear traffic all night."

"So key or no key?"

She met his gaze and held it. "Are you really sure you want me in your life? I'm a mess."

"Babe, you're not a mess. You have history. I have shit in my life that bugs me."

She took a bite of food and moaned. "This is good. So what has been bugging you?"

He swallowed his food then took a sip of tea. "The military is harsh on couples. When injuries happen, it's even harsher. A few of my friends are going through shit, and I guess I'm taking too much of their problems on. I get all wrapped up in my head, wondering if you'll stay if something happens to me. I know it hasn't even happened, and I'm way overthinking, but it affects my mood."

Sunshine put down her fork and reached for him, laying her hand on his arm. "If I make a commitment to you, that's it. We're together. You end up missing a leg or an arm, we'll figure it out."

"If? How close are you to making a commitment?"

Sunshine took another bite and concentrated on the table. After she swallowed, she spoke without looking up. "I still think you're crazy for wanting to be with me. My brother could come back and try to kill me. He's not a good man, and—"

"But you're a good person. I don't care about him. I care about you."

She closed her eyes and shook her head. Minx moved to her side and pulled her into his arms. She plastered her body against his and clung to him like he was the last floating piece of driftwood, and she was drowning in an ocean with no land in sight.

He kissed the top of her head while she cried. After a moment, he sat down and settled her on his lap, feeding her and himself from the same plate. When they finished his food, he pulled her plate close and fed them, not wanting to let go of her.

After they finished eating, she tried to stand, but he held her in place. "I want you to understand I don't judge you based on what someone else did to you. You aren't at fault."

"I feel like I was."

"But you weren't. How much older is your brother than you?"

"Seven years."

"By the time I was eighteen, I had a gun and was making life or death decisions. Your brother was old enough to know what he was doing was wrong. He took advantage of you, and he has kept taking advantage of you. You are not at fault. I know that's easy for me to say and harder for you to accept, but I want you to realize you are blameless in this."

Sunshine blew out a breath. "I think it's time I found a therapist here. I know what you are saying is true, but I need help keeping that thought in my head."

"A therapist would be good. I should talk to one, too. I know I'm not at fault for what happened to my buddies, but survivors' guilt is real."

Sunshine kissed his cheek then moved to kiss his lips. After a moment, she straddled him, and he slunk down in the chair, so her weight was on his cock. He wanted to be inside her, but she'd worn pants today, and he couldn't just slip her panties to the side to fuck her.

"I need you," Minx whispered when the kiss ended.

Sunshine stood and undid her pants before shoving them to the floor. She tugged off her underwear and then removed her shirt and bra. She stood in front of him, totally naked and inviting.

Heat whipped through him, making him incredibly hard. This woman did it for him. He never wanted to lose her.

He reached out and trailed his fingers over the curve of her hip before tracing a path up to her breasts. He pinched one nipple then the other before reaching between her legs. She widened her stance, giving him room to touch and explore.

His fingers found her clit, and he flicked and rubbed, taking her higher. Her body shook, and he moved fast, pulling her into his lap. His thumb rubbed on her clit while he slid two fingers into her wet heat.

She arched up and cried out just before her pussy clamped down on his fingers. As she pulsed around him, he closed his eyes, thankful he had her in his life.

While she rested on him, he undid his pants and pulled his cock out. He moved her to straddle him and eased her down on his length. Her eyes rolled up in her head as she sank down on him, sighing when he filled her.

He lifted and lowered her, enjoying the sensation

of her wet heat around his cock. He was so close to orgasm when his eyes flashed open.

"Fuck, condom." Minx pulled her off and stood in one swift motion. "I'm so sorry. I can't forget condoms."

"Let's go to your room and finish this."

He would have understood if she'd walked out on him, but she led him down the hall and into his room, her ass swaying as she walked, mesmerizing him totally. She pushed him to the bed and sucked him until he was hard again, then rolled a condom over his length before sinking down on him.

He was still fully dressed, just his cock sticking out of the front of his pants, and she was totally naked. The visual of her riding him like a pro seared in his mind and took him higher. She rocked and rolled her hips, making him see stars as she fucked herself on him. When she lowered and bit his nipple through the material of his shirt, he cried out and almost came.

Then Sunshine sat up and grabbed her breasts, tugging on her nipples. Watching her pleasure herself was enough to push him over the edge. He came hard into the condom, half wishing he hadn't remembered protection. He loved how hot and wet she'd been on his dick and wanted that again. But that came after trust, and he needed her to trust him.

After finishing her orgasm, she dropped to the bed beside him. When she closed her eyes, he studied her face, drinking in her features. She made him feel alive, like he could take on the world and do everything needed to win in life. With her beside him, he was whole.

CHAPTER 7

Sunshine stood at the door of the closet she'd taken over in Ethan's house. Half her clothes were here, and she wondered if she should keep the small apartment she'd rented when she moved to Hawaii.

"Hey, there you are," Ethan said as he stepped into the room.

She turned and narrowed her gaze. She had to admit he was a beast of a man. He looked absolutely amazing, and she still couldn't believe he wanted her.

"Half my clothes are here."

"Maybe your other clothes are lonely, and you need to get them."

Laughter bubbled up, and she moved to him,

happy he knew how to make her feel good. "You're a funny one. Are you sure you want this?"

"What, you living with me? It has nearly been a full month since you moved your toothbrush and the first piece of clothing in here. I think it's time you accept that you're living here with me."

"What if you get bored with me or decide—"

"Nope. We're not playing that game. I'm not going to get bored with you. We do more than have sex. Think about that hike we went on, the days we've spent just hanging out, or going to the beach with our friends. Our relationship isn't shallow."

She shook her head. "No, it's not. I actually like you." Ethan chuckled at her statement. "I didn't mean anything bad."

He laughed harder. "I know what you mean. I like you. I mean really like, not just love."

"Wait, you love me?"

Ethan rolled his eyes. "Duh. I fell in love with you fast, but I like you as a friend. You're awesome and fun. And I like spending time with you."

She wrapped her arms around his waist, resting her head against his chest, listening to his strong heartbeat. She loved listening to him breathe and the thud-thud of his heart. He kissed the top of her head, and she sighed. She could stay like this forever.

Maybe not exactly like this, but she loved how good he felt up against her.

His phone buzzed, and he pulled it out and stiffened. Worry filled her. He hadn't had to rush out of the country yet, but she knew it was coming.

"What's up?"

"Ashley just had the baby."

"What? I thought they were going to call when they went to the hospital."

"Well, Wig got home, and she was in the shower. She said she didn't feel good. The next thing he knew, she was squatting and screaming."

"You and your nicknames. You'd think I was used to them, but I'm so not."

Ethan chuckled. "Still can't think of me as Minx?"

She rolled her eyes, and he buzzed her cheek with his lips. He turned the phone so she could see a photo of the baby that looked like it had just been squeezed out of a pipe. There was blood and other things that would make most guys squeamish, but Ethan and his team weren't most guys.

His phone buzzed again and he checked the text. "The ambulance just arrived. They're going to the hospital."

"Damn. That woman just squatted in the shower

and gave birth. I want her on my team if we play any sports games."

Ethan laughed again. "Sports games? You're too funny."

"You know what I mean."

"I do. She's badass. Like legit hardcore."

"So are we going to see the baby or waiting?"

Ethan checked his phone again. "He said to wait. Ashley needs some sleep."

Sunshine's phone rang, and she moved across the room to grab it. The display showed Jenna's name.

"Hello, Jenna."

"Hey, we're going over to clean up Ashley's place. I don't want her coming home to a mess."

"Sure. Give me a sec." Sunshine turned to Ethan. "We're going over to clean up Ashley's house."

"Let me change, and I'll drive you over."

"You don't—"

"Yes, I do."

Sunshine shrugged and lifted her phone to her ear. "Ethan is coming, too."

"Good. So is Vine. We should be able to get everything picked up and cleaned fast."

Sunshine sighed. These people really were good. "This is a great idea."

"I can't imagine giving birth in the shower. At least Wig was there," Jenna said.

Sunshine nodded as she found her shoes and pulled them on. "Right? She's a badass."

"She is," Jenna said. "I wonder how I'll handle it. I don't know if I could be so calm and not freak out."

"I'm sure you'll do great," Sunshine said as she stepped out of the house with Ethan.

"I'm going to let you go. I'll see you in a bit," Jenna said before ending the call.

As they made their way over to his vehicle, a twig or something snapped behind her. The hair on the back of her neck went up, and she spun.

"Everything okay?" Ethan asked.

She pushed away the weird feeling and turned to face him. "Yeah. I just thought I heard something. It's nothing. Probably a bird."

Ethan narrowed his eyes as he stared into the bushes but didn't say more. He opened the vehicle door for her and got her into the car before he headed over to the bushes and the side of the house. She felt ridiculous for making him go over there. She shouldn't have said anything. No one was following her. She didn't need to freak out over some animal making noise.

After a few seconds, Ethan was back and getting

into the vehicle, a frown turning his lips down. "I didn't see anything."

"It's nothing."

He huffed out a breath and shook his head. "It's not always nothing when you hear something like that. Don't discount your internal warning system."

She shook her head. "I just can't live my life looking over my shoulder all the time."

"Your right, but I'm here to look for you. I'll make sure no one is lurking around once we get home."

"How will you do that?"

"The ground is still damp from all the rain. If they left tracks, I'll find them. For now, let's just concentrate on making Ashley's life easier."

The drive was short, and before she knew it, they were about a block from Ashley's place. Excitement filled her. "I can't wait to see the little guy."

"He looked healthy. I haven't received any other notes about the baby. I'm sure if there was something wrong, Wig would send out a note.

When they arrived at Ashley's house, the gang was already there. Two of the guys were mowing the lawn, taking care of the outside of the house, so Robert didn't have to when they came home.

"Hey, Minx, Sunshine," Vine called out from the porch. "The women are inside putting fresh sheets on their bed. I think we've cleaned up most of the mess. It really was just contained to the shower."

"That's good," Ethan said.

"I can't believe she had the baby in the shower." Vine shook his head. "She's one tough cookie."

Sunshine gave him a hug as she passed by. She couldn't believe this was her life now. She had friends who were close. All the guys on Ethan's team and their women were friends. She'd always tried to maintain a distance before, but these people didn't know the meaning of the word distance.

"Hey, Sunshine," Jenna called out as she entered the room.

"Hey yourself. How about I clean the toilets and make sure their trash is emptied."

"Sure," Becky said. "We're almost done in here."

Sunshine looked around, taking in the clean room. "I'm sure they'll appreciate a clean house when they get home. That baby was due yesterday, and I know they were ready, but wow, can you imagine having it so fast that an ambulance couldn't even make it?"

"She must have been in labor for a few hours," Jenna said.

"Yeah, she probably was." Becky slid the pillow into the case and then tossed it on the bed.

Sunshine stepped into the bathroom and looked under the sink for cleaner. It was at the back of the cabinet. She cleaned the toilet and sink then emptied the trash into the larger bin in the kitchen.

Becky and Forest ran to the store to pick up a few items for the couple. By the time they got back, she had both bathrooms clean. Someone had vacuumed the floor and mopped the tile. The place sparkled.

"It looks great," Ethan said.

"It does. I'll let Wig know his house is clean," Vine said.

All of the guys' phones dinged, and they all flinched a little. Then they smiled. Ethan turned his phone so she could see more photos of Ashley, the baby, and Robert.

"Aw, they look so happy," Jenna said.

"They do," Vine said. "I have to say I'm glad that wasn't a command to come to base. I know if we're called, we'll all go, but I don't want to miss the first few weeks of their kid's life."

"Anyone know what they are naming him?" Sunshine asked.

"No clue," Jenna said.

"They were keeping it a secret," Becky said.

"I wonder why," Quirk asked.

Sunshine didn't know why she didn't know all their first names. She knew Wig was Robert, and Legs was Anthony, but she wasn't really sure of the rest of the guys. The kids would have an interesting time learning everyone's name.

"That baby is going to be well taken care of, but my goodness, he's going to have a hard time remembering all of your names. What with you all having multiple names." They all turned to stare at her and then burst out laughing.

"We do go by multiple names," Ethan said. "But we're patient with people who don't remember."

She nodded. "You are."

"The kid is going to have so many people looking out for him," Vine said.

Jenna placed a hand on her rounded belly. "It's exciting raising a kid in this huge group."

"We're going to spoil them rotten," Quirk said.

"And teach them to be respectable," added Legs.

"Best leave that to others." Astro kept a straight face for about five seconds until Legs started in on him.

"Wait, are you saying I'm not respectable? I'm plenty respectable." Legs followed Astro out the front door.

Before the door shut, she heard Astro say, "Not

from what I saw the last time we went dancing at that bar."

Ethan leaned in close. "They're just joking with each other. They're good guys."

Sunshine chuckled. "I'm sure they've gotten themselves into plenty of interesting situations at bars."

"Don't get them started on stories," Jenna said.

"Otherwise, we'll be here all night," Becky added.

"They think they're unique, but they're just like all the other guys out there when it comes to bar stories," Jenna said.

"Hey, we are unique," Quirk said.

Jenna patted him on the head like a parent would with a preschooler. "Sure you are, honey. Sure you are."

Everyone laughed. It was refreshing being with this group. They knew how to have a good time together and how to be friends. It had been hard to make and keep friends when she'd been younger because of her brother and his overbearing attitude. Add to it the fact that her parents moved all the time, which meant few people got close to her. She'd attended so many different schools she couldn't remember them all.

"Hey, you okay?" Ethan asked.

She met his gaze and smiled, fighting tears that started filling her eyes. "Yeah. I'm happy I met you. It's different from what I'm used to. I like this."

He pulled her close and kissed the top of her head, then her cheek. He gave her a look that told her once they got home, he was going to make sure she knew how much he cared for her.

Luck seemed to be on her side. Since coming to Hawaii and meeting Ethan, it seemed like nothing could go wrong. Any happiness she'd known before paled in comparison to what she felt now. Being with Ethan and this group had changed her, given her hope, and allowed her to dream again.

CHAPTER 8

Minx blew out a breath then jumped, enjoying the rush of air before he hit the crystal-clear water. They were doing a training exercise with Mustang's team. He was one of the last guys to drop into the water. They were off the coast of Kauai, heading to shore. Once on land, they had forty-five minutes to make it to a location where they would call in and be picked up by the helicopter that dropped them.

Being in the open ocean without a boat nearby had been scary at first. As a kid, the idea of being a SEAL had appealed to him though he'd never been in the ocean before. Then he'd joined the Navy, planning on becoming a SEAL. The first time out in the sea, he'd almost had a panic attack. He'd hidden the fact, not wanting others to know he couldn't handle the open ocean.

Now, the water was like his second home. He'd leaned into the fear, pushing at the panic until it no longer bothered him. Sharks loved Hawaii, but he didn't think about the great whites that swam in these waters because it wouldn't do him any good. He knew how to handle himself in the ocean now, and for that, he was eternally grateful.

He made it to shore and spotted Midas, Alec, Pid, and Vine. He dropped low and glanced down the beach, seeing four other members of his team coming in. During training, they had spotters in the air watching to make sure everyone made it to shore. On a live mission, if something happened, it happened, and they would mourn their brother once they got home. It took a bit of time to come to terms with potential loss, though. Sure, they helped each other when they could, but each man was responsible for himself. If he thought he couldn't perform at the top of his game, he sidelined himself. Being sidelined when he'd been sick had sucked. No question, he would take care of himself so he didn't have to deal with sitting out again.

Once his buddies were accounted for, they started moving toward the exfil position. They had to tag themselves in at certain locations, indicating they'd accomplished their tasks. It wasn't as difficult as a live mission would have been, but exercises like this kept them fresh.

On the sandy beach they had little cover and had to move fast. Once at the tree line, they relaxed a little but still had to stay on guard as they made their way through the bushy trees.

"You ever wonder why they have us run this during the day?" Pid asked.

"No," Mustang said.

"I mean, we're so visible it's crazy."

"Jesus, Pid, just shut up and do the exercise," Slate barked.

"Just trying to make the time go faster," Pid replied.

"It's not working," Slate said.

Minx laughed with the rest of the guys. He loved the guys on his team and got on well with the men from the other teams here in Hawaii. They worked well together, which made life easier. With Astro leaving the team, he prayed it didn't change their dynamic too much.

A small noise sounded off to their left. Vine lifted his hand, signaling they should stop moving. Minx and Legs circled around, moving silently through the trees to check on the noise.

When they'd gone about twenty feet, they found two men trying to spring a trap on them. Minx signaled he would take out the one on the right, and Legs took the other one. They moved with speed but no noise, tagging the men on the shoulder. That meant they were out of the game. Minx and Legs headed back to their unit and told Vine they were clear.

They moved silently to their final location. Once they tagged in, everyone relaxed.

Legs sat down next to Minx. "Everything going well with your girlfriend?"

Minx shrugged. "Her family is concerning."

"Concerning how?"

Minx wiped his hand over his face. "It's complicated. Her brother is bad business. We can't find him, and I don't like it."

"You know we have resources for stuff like this." Mustang came up behind him and put his hand on Minx's shoulder.

He turned and met his friend's gaze. "Tex has been on it for a while."

Mustang's eyebrows shot up. "If Tex can't find him, then the dude has gone deep."

Minx nodded. "That's why I'm worried."

Midas moved closer. "I'm seeing Rawlins later today. Maybe you should talk to him. I can ask if he can get involved."

Minx felt weird asking Rawlins for help. The guy was a good man, but he worried about Rawlins taking on too much for them.

"He likes to help," Mustang said.

Minx shrugged then bumped fists with Midas. "If he agrees to it. I don't want him to feel like he has to."

Mustang chuckled. "Trust me, Rawlins isn't going to do anything he doesn't want to."

A little weight lifted off Minx but he still felt the twist of unease at not knowing where Sunshine's brother was. Maybe the guy was losing himself in some remote forest, but Minx feared he was still searching for Sunshine.

They caught their helicopter back to Oahu, all of them happy with their performance. Before Midas left for the day, he came by and got information about Sepher.

"I'll call if Rawlins wants to meet," Midas said.

Minx bumped Midas's fist. "Thanks. I trust you."

Midas winked, then pulled him in for a bro hug.

"Dude, we have to look out for each other. I'll call you later."

Minx headed home, worried that he'd opened up too much. None of the guys other than maybe Vine knew how bad it was for Sunshine, and he didn't want to break her trust by exposing how awful Sepher had been. The guy deserved to die and he wished he could be the person to end Sepher's life. Sunshine needed to be free from the threat of her brother. He just hoped she wasn't upset another person was looking into Sepher's whereabouts.

CHAPTER 9

Sunshine dropped to the couch and closed her eyes. Her last shift had been crazy. A guy had attacked the receptionist when someone had dropped a metal bowl in the hall. Sunshine had to hold him down until a security guard had shown up. By then, she'd talked him down, and he was apologetic about reacting to the noise.

It sucked how many military men and women suffered from trauma. Their lives were forever changed because they chose to join the military. She knew everyone made choices, and they had to live with the outcomes, but she wished the military made it easier for people suffering to get help. The military was trying, but for many it was too little too late.

Now the man who'd attacked their receptionist would end up with some sort of punishment. It wasn't cool to go around attacking people, but it also wasn't cool he'd had to work to get help for a problem caused by his job.

She let out a heavy sigh, pushing thoughts of the office to the back of her mind. She still felt like someone was watching her. A part of her wanted to look deeper, but Ethan had a friend keeping an eye out for Sepher. She was in the clear. Her brother hadn't shown up anywhere, and he wasn't watching her. She could let it go and just enjoy life.

The door opened, and Sunshine didn't crack her eyes open. "I'm exhausted. Bad day at the office."

"You never should have run."

The voice sent panic through Sunshine. Her eyes flew open as her breath caught in her throat. She tried to get air but coughing erupted instead. Her feet moved, but her body didn't. She half-stumbled, half-crawled over the back of the couch, and tried to run to the right but got tangled up in the pair of sweats Ethan had dropped on the back of the couch before he'd left this morning and she'd pushed off in her rush to escape.

"You know better than to run from me." Sepher

stalked closer, his beady eyes stayed on her as he moved closer. Fear slid through her and her stomach clenched.

"Leave." Sunshine hated how her voice shook. She wanted to be stronger, but this man brought out the worst of her fears.

Her brother's laughter sent chills through her. No way would he leave without her. If Ethan came home, Sepher would kill him. There wasn't any other way around this. She had to go with her brother. She could try to stall, but she would never forgive herself if something happened to Ethan.

"What are you doing here?" Sunshine asked, still trying to find an escape but knowing there wasn't one. Sepher would have already planned for her to run.

"You know why I'm here. I'm here for what is mine. You and I are going to go have a little fun together."

Sunshine made a dash for the door, but Sepher was too quick. He reached out and shoved her. She fell to the ground, her hands slapping hard on the floor to stop her face from crashing into the tiles.

He grabbed her hair and yanked, pulling out a bunch as he held her head up. Tears sprang to her eyes. Once he had her, he wouldn't ever let her go. There was no way she would escape him.

He held her head up, sending pain down her back and legs. "I have metal cuffs for you this time."

She shook her head, wishing she had run farther. "Leave me alone."

"You're mine, and no one can have you," Sepher yelled in her ear, bringing another wave of pain and nausea.

She tried to get away and had made it a few inches before he forced her to turn and face him. He punched her in the face then the chest. He was stronger and meaner. He grabbed one wrist and slapped on the cuffs. Tears gathered in her eyes.

He forced her up and then yanked her other arm behind her back and slapped on the second cuff. There was no way she could get free.

The sound of an engine cutting off in the driveway gave her hope. But her hope was dashed when Sepher grabbed a baseball bat and moved to the entryway. She didn't want to scream before Ethan came in because he would rush in to save her. She waited until she heard the door open, and then she yelled a warning.

"Duck!"

She prayed Ethan jumped out of the way. She feared he would be caught in Sepher's trap. She heard the thud of the bat, followed by a lot of cursing and scrambling. Something crashed to the floor, and then she heard the bat make contact with something that sounded human.

"Oh God." Her voice caught in her throat and she only made a squeak.

Sunshine rolled and awkwardly made her way to her feet. She shuffled to the entryway and saw Ethan on the ground. She tried to run to him, but Sepher grabbed her by her hair and yanked her away from her lover. She cried out, begging for him to help Ethan. Sepher only laughed.

"He'll be dead soon. Too bad we can't stick around and watch him die."

Sepher pulled her close and held up a roll of gray duct tape. She fought him, but he trapped her against the wall as he secured the tape over her mouth. On the walk out to the car, he had to hold her close to keep her from dropping to the ground. She tried every trick to get away, but it wasn't enough. Sepher's hold was too tight, and she had no way to get free.

He forced her into the trunk and slammed the

lid. Her fear was off the charts, bringing tears to her eyes.

The engine turned over, and she tried to scream, but the tape muffled her cries for help. She heard something hit the trunk lid, but the vehicle sped away, leaving behind the only man she'd ever loved.

CHAPTER 10

Minx had made it outside and tried to get to Sunshine, but the guy took off with his girlfriend. Minx at least had the sense to pull out his phone and take a few pictures as the car drove away.

The world spun, and he dropped to the ground. A minute, or maybe it was only a few seconds later, someone tugged on his shoulder, asking him a million questions, or what felt like a million. His head pounded, and he wanted to throw up, but he had to keep it together for Sunshine.

"Call the police," Minx got out before the world went dim again.

Hands held him up and tapped his cheek. He growled, or thought he did, and the person next to him tightened their hold.

"Hang in there."

"He has her," Minx mumbled.

"Who?" the voice asked.

"Her brother." Minx gasped for breath. Talking hurt. "He's going to kill her."

Pain filled Minx, and he pulled out his phone, somehow managing to send the photos of the car to the group text with the guys and then typed in 911. They would know something was wrong. The pain was too much, and he passed out again, waking when the ambulance arrived.

He tried to talk, but pain messed up his words. He thought he'd gotten out that his girlfriend had been kidnapped, but he might have been talking rubbish.

The sound of beeping woke him. His eyes flashed open. Pain seared the back of his brain. He regretted opening his eyes.

"Hey, they've already looked at your brain, your skull isn't fractured, but you have a concussion," Vine said.

"Shit. Where is Sunshine?" His voice sounded like he'd swallowed a razor.

"We don't know yet. But Midas was with Rawlins when your text was delivered to me, and I sent it on to them. They are on this."

He relaxed against the pillow, knowing he wouldn't be of any use until the pain lowered and the room stopped spinning.

"I feel like shit," Minx mumbled.

"Yeah. You were hit hard. Your arm is bruised, no bones broken."

He grunted and sat up more, blinking open his eyes again. "I freaking hate her brother."

"Same," Vine said. "We'll get her back. He can't hide from us or our resources."

"He hid from Tex and somehow made his way here."

"Tex feels bad about that. Her brother has a bunch of fake IDs. Now that he's stuck his head up, Tex has found two of those IDs that allowed him to hide. We'll track down the rest of his names and figure out where the jerk has been hiding. We'll also figure out how to get Sunshine back."

Minx wanted to cry. He wanted to rant and rave at the injustice of Sunshine being taken from him. The anger swirling inside made his head hurt more.

"I was out for weeks before, now I'm going to be out of commission again. I'm going to lose my spot as a SEAL. I hate this."

"Hey, it's not your fault. I know it sucks, but you're not losing your spot. I'll make sure of that."

Minx closed his eyes and tried to fight the tears. Late at night, when they'd been tangled together in the sheets after making love, Sunshine had expressed to him how afraid she was of her brother. He'd abused her to the point he left permanent scars on her psyche and her body. She deserved better than to be trapped with the jerk.

Minx didn't deserve her if he couldn't keep her safe. Guilt filled him. He would do better if she ever came back to him.

"Listen to me," Vine said. "This isn't your fault. I know you're blaming yourself. Don't. Get better, and let's go after her. The guys are searching, the cops are looking, Rawlins has people on it. We will find her."

Minx blew out a breath, hating that he was in the hospital, unable to help. "I need to get up and get—"

Vine put his hand on Minx's chest, holding him down. "You need to get better, and that means you don't get up and try to leave until the doctor dismisses you."

He blew out a breath as he flopped back onto the bed. "This is bullshit."

"Yep. It's total bullshit. That's why I'm here. To make sure you follow the total bullshit the doctor prescribed and don't try to leave until they say it's okay."

Minx hated that he'd been hurt again, but he was livid that Sunshine had been taken. He'd give up everything, even being a SEAL to have Sunshine back. That realization was sobering. He couldn't probe the thought too much, or he might lose his mind. He wanted her back with him, which meant getting out of the hospital. He needed to find Sunshine and make sure she was safe.

Doctors and nurses came in and left, not saying much. About four hours later, he was allowed to go home, with restrictions. He couldn't drive, was told not to watch movies or TV, and to keep his activity low for a few days. He had an appointment to see the doctor again in a week. His concussion wasn't too bad, but they wanted to make sure he was all clear before they sent him into a war zone.

Minx didn't say anything to Vine in the car and was still in a bad mood when they entered his house. Legs was on a computer, and Wig was on another one sitting in his kitchen.

"What are you two doing here?" Minx barked.

"We're looking for his car. Thanks to Rawlins and a little help from Tex, we have access to the city's cameras. We're searching right now. It's hard to find a single car in this mess. We haven't seen him yet, but we're not giving up."

Minx headed to the kitchen and grabbed a glass from the cabinet. Moving to the sink seemed automatic, but the rage inside built, and he tossed the glass across the room instead of filling it with water. The glass didn't smash into a million pieces. Instead, it bounced off the wall and then rolled to a stop at Vine's feet.

Vine cocked up his eyebrows. "Dude, breaking glass won't bring her back."

Minx closed his eyes and tried to get the anger under control. "I failed her."

"No. Her brother is a psychopath—"

"And I'm supposed to protect her."

Vine's hand landed on his shoulder. He wanted to brush off the hold, but he didn't. He blew out a breath before he met Vine's gaze.

"Bad things happen. That's just how life is. We'll find her and get her back."

Minx swallowed over the lump in his throat. "I want to kill him."

"I know. But we're in the USA. We can't kill him. It wouldn't look right. Someone would get pissed."

"Fuck."

"Yeah, I know. Fuck." Vine set the glass Minx had

thrown in the sink then grabbed another one, filling it with water. "Drink this. Then we'll get you settled in the den and tell you everything we've done."

"I want to go look for her," Minx said.

"I know. But you can't drive, and I need to be here helping look at cameras."

He threw up his arms. "This seems so pointless."

"What we do often seems pointless, but it isn't. You know that."

His frustrated sigh filled the kitchen. "I can't do nothing."

"You're getting better. That's something. Let us look. I know it's not what you want to do, but I need to get back in there and search all the cameras. There are too many feeds to look at, and we don't have enough resources."

Minx met Vine's gaze and gave a sharp nod. He couldn't help with the videos because he couldn't focus enough on the screen to make out the license plate numbers. He was keeping Vine from doing what needed to be done. Minx gave a sharp nod, then moved to the couch and rested his head against the cushions with his eyes closed, listening to his friends talk as they searched.

He drifted off at one point and woke to an empty room. The pit of despair he felt seemed insurmountable. He had fallen hard for Sunshine, wanted her with him all the time, and now she had disappeared. He wanted her back.

"Fuck!"

Vine stepped into the room, his eyebrows raised. "What's going on?"

Minx rolled his eyes. "Nothing other than my world falling apart."

"I know it seems like we aren't making progress but we will."

A pit opened in his chest, leaving him empty. "I just want her back."

Vine nodded. "I know."

He looked up, meeting Vine's gaze. "What am I going to do?"

"Get well, and then we'll take down her brother. He can't hide from us forever."

Vine didn't say anything. They both knew the violence of people like Sunshine's brother. If his anger didn't get the best of him in the beginning, it would take over in a few months, weeks, or days. She had a limited window of survivability. She could already be dead if Sepher had a break from reality.

Minx prayed she wasn't gone. They needed a miracle. He just didn't know if he would get it.

CHAPTER 11

Three long days had passed since he'd gotten out of the hospital. His head still hurt a little, but he was able to sit at the computer for a few minutes. He searched for any sign of Sepher or Sunshine to no avail.

The other guys were out looking when they weren't at work. Rawlins hadn't stopped. He had a couple of guys on the island keeping tabs at the marinas, but so far, they hadn't found anything.

Minx let loose a growl of frustration as the pain behind his eyes grew. He stepped away from the computer, knowing he had to keep looking or he might miss something, but he couldn't keep going. He had to rest his eyes and his head.

His phone rang, and hope bubbled up but died when he saw Vine's name. "Hey," Minx said.

"We're getting off early. I'll be at your house in thirty minutes. The rest of the guys are splitting up and driving around the island."

"You all are the best friends in the world."

"Dude, we'd die for you. This is a small thing. I know we haven't found her yet, but we will."

Minx didn't want to tell Vine his hopes had been dashed so many times in the last few days he didn't think hope was real. After ending the call, he grabbed some water and over-the-counter medicine for his headache then returned to the computer, vowing to stay longer at the screen.

The search seemed just as fruitless as before. A car door shut out front, and he checked his watch, seeing about thirty minutes had passed since Vine had called. His door was unlocked, and he knew Vine would come in. He closed his eyes for a moment, then opened them, forcing his vision to focus on the action on the computer.

He blinked, then blinked again as a woman who looked like Sunshine stepped into a store. She looked frantic. The door opened behind her, and sure enough, Sepher stepped in and grabbed her arm. The way Sepher jerked her close, the frown on his face, and how he leaned in showed his malice. Sunshine was in deep trouble, and if they didn't find her soon, she wouldn't survive.

"Hey, I'm—" Vine stopped behind him then bent closer, staring at the screen. "Where is that?"

Minx checked the information for the video he was watching. "Looks to be a store near Kahuku Beach."

"When is this from?"

Minx clicked the feed. "Five-minute delay."

Vine tapped him on the shoulder. "Put on your shoes. Let's go."

Minx couldn't believe they had found her. Sepher had to be keeping her over on that side of the island. It had been a long time since he'd driven over to the Kahuku area. They had a few thousand people in Kahuku. He hoped someone had seen them and would reveal where Sepher was keeping Sunshine.

Vine put the phone on speaker as they settled in his truck. "Hey, Rawlins. We found her. She's in Kahuku."

The sound of Rawlins' vehicle slowing played over the speaker. "Let me check…it's about fifty minutes from where I am."

"We're driving that way. She was at the store off the highway and Puuluana Street. Maybe the clerk knows where they are staying. I'll call the rest of the crew and tell them to head that way."

Minx's hands shook as he strapped in for the drive. This was as close as they'd come to finding her in the last few days. Excitement filled him. She would be home with him soon. At least he hoped she would.

The rest of the guys were making their way to Kahuku. The drive seemed to take forever. Legs called and said he and Astro were in the area, driving up and down streets. Wig sent a message, stating that he and Quirk were going to the store to ask questions. They vowed they would find Sunshine today.

By the time Vine and Minx got there, Rawlins had found out Sunshine and Sepher were in a house at the edge of town. They made their way to the location. They should call the cops, but the police would take forever to get here. Any police stationed here in Kahuku wouldn't have enough people to handle Sepher. He didn't want Sunshine injured in the crossfire because there weren't enough cops to properly take down Sepher.

Just as they were about to move to surround the house, the back door opened and banged closed.

"What was that?" Minx asked.

Legs moved around the side of the house, calling back to them. "Guy, taking off." Legs gave chase, followed by Astro.

Minx wanted to go with them, but he had to find Sunshine. He headed into the house, calling out as he moved from room to room. He didn't hear anything for a long time, then he finally heard a muffled cry.

He opened a closet and found Sunshine on the floor, her hands and legs bound with something stuffed in her mouth. He pulled the cloth away from her mouth, and she sucked in a huge breath.

"Oh God, Minx. You're alive."

"Babe." Tears filled his eyes, and he pulled her close.

The sound of a siren close by sent panic through him. He prayed Rawlins could take care of this. They didn't need their CO finding out they'd come all the way over here to take on Sunshine's kidnapper.

An ambulance showed up. The two female paramedics seemed to know their stuff as they checked out Sunshine. They were talking about taking Sunshine to the hospital, but she declined transport.

"Are you sure?" one of the paramedics asked.

"I'm good. He didn't really hurt me this time. No beatings. I just want to go home and rest."

The cop leaned in, his expression serious. "They need to do a rape kit on you."

Sunshine paled, and for a moment, Minx thought she would throw up.

"I'll be there for you," Minx said.

The cop shot him a sideways glance then huffed in disgust. "You should be glad Rawlins was with you. You all can't go all enforc—"

"I'm sure Rawlins explained that we were just over here and had no clue Sunshine was in this house," Minx said.

The officer rolled his eyes and huffed out a breath. "Good God. For an excuse, that's thin. Seriously, get better excuses next time, or just don't do this next time."

The cop stalked off after telling Sunshine she needed to head to the hospital. She didn't look happy as she rolled her eyes and sat back on the stretcher.

"Fine, I'll go," Sunshine said.

"Good. We'll get you there in one piece," the paramedic said.

Sunshine's eyebrows pinched together. "I hope so."

The paramedic chuckled. "I'm a comedian in my off time."

The other paramedic shook her head. "Be thankful I'm the one riding in the back with you. I'll keep you safe and not crack any terrible jokes."

"I'll see you there," Minx said as they strapped Sunshine in.

The ambulance took off, and Minx felt like he'd lost an arm or some other part of his body. He desperately needed to be with Sunshine.

Vine came up behind him and clapped him on the back. "Let's go. I know you want to see her."

The ambulance wasn't taking her far. The medical center was on the other side of town, just a few miles away from the house where Sepher had kept Sunshine. The police were on the case now, but Rawlins said he would keep looking for information on Sunshine's brother. The man had escaped, but he couldn't hide forever. They would find him soon enough. And when they did, Minx would make sure the man paid dearly for everything he'd put Sunshine through.

CHAPTER 12

The last few days had been hell. Sepher had been more unhinged than usual. He'd stopped taking whatever meds he'd been on before. Now her brother's irrational mind was left to run wild. He'd said some scary stuff while he held her. Sepher might be involved with a cult, maybe. She didn't want to see him again and find out, though.

"We're almost finished here," the doctor said.

The door opened, and Ethan stepped in. Sadness filled Sunshine. She didn't want Ethan involved in Sepher's madness. She'd known she couldn't get close to anyone. That only drew them into the fire, which meant Sepher won.

"Your head. How is it?"

Ethan moved close to her and shook his head. “I’m fine. No lasting damage. I just need to rest for a few more days.”

Sunshine swallowed, trying to keep from crying as she watched Ethan, searching for the lie in his words. He wasn’t okay. There was much more to Sepher beating Ethan than he was letting on.

She didn’t want her brother destroying the best man she’d ever known. No question, she couldn’t stay with Ethan. He would try to protect her, but there was no protecting her from Sepher. Her brother was unhinged and would try to take her again, maybe killing Ethan the next time.

The doctor left the room, and Ethan sat in the chair next to her, holding her hand. He didn’t say anything, which she appreciated. She would have to break up with him soon. The idea of calling off her relationship with Ethan hurt. She didn’t want to end this, but she had few choices.

If Sepher came back, he would kill Ethan. Her brother wouldn’t stop until he had her again. She doubted the cops would catch Ethan. He wasn’t stupid, but he was off his medicine and irrational. Maybe he’d make a big enough mistake the police could swoop in and take him.

Vine drove them home, leaving them alone after making sure they were both okay. She hadn't said anything about ending their relationship yet. She didn't want the confrontation. She hated confrontation. Maybe she would just grab her clothes and leave.

Ethan pulled her close and held her. They fit together so nicely. Being in Minx's arms was heaven. She wanted to be with him but knew it would be impossible.

Once Sepher realized how close she was to Ethan, he would sabotage everything. If Ethan got hurt, it would ruin her. She wanted her boyfriend to stay healthy and safe. That meant she had to leave.

Maybe she could find a job somewhere outside of the USA. Sepher would eventually ruin everything, though. He wasn't going to give up. She needed to change her name, but then she would have to change her nursing license. Heck, she would have to change all her documentation.

She stood at the sink in the bathroom, trying to come to terms with the need to leave Ethan. He wouldn't let her go easily. She would have to hurt him bad. But how could she do that? He would see the truth in her eyes if she did it face to face. No, she would have to just not show up for a while and then send him a note saying they were over. If she looked into his eyes, he would see how desperate she was for him.

A knock sounded on the bathroom door. "Hey, are you ready for something to eat? Or do you just want to go to bed?"

He'd been so nice, not asking exactly what happened. He didn't need to know the details. The marks on her body told the story.

"I'm not hungry. I'll be out in a moment."

She couldn't face him, not knowing she was going to walk out. God, this was so hard. Tears filled her eyes and traced down her cheeks. She needed to protect Ethan. Sepher was pure evil, which meant she was tainted. She couldn't put Ethan through more of her crap. He had to be saved, and the only way to save him was to leave.

After drying her eyes, she stepped out of the bathroom, wishing she'd asked to be dropped off at her apartment. Ethan sat in the den, looking so kind and wonderful it broke her heart.

An uneasy feeling slid through her as he pulled her into a hug. She hated herself for planning to leave. She was an albatross, but he probably wouldn't listen. If she stayed with him, his life would be ruined. Already he'd suffered from Sepher. She couldn't allow him to suffer more.

She tried not to be too obvious, but she caught Ethan giving her strange looks. She guessed she wasn't doing a great job acting normal. Bedtime couldn't come soon enough.

When Ethan left for work the next day, she would pack up all her things and leave. She couldn't put him through more suffering. It was the best thing to do. He needed to be protected, even if he didn't think so.

The next morning, Ethan pulled her close, and she went willingly, wishing she could experience this with him forever. But she wasn't lucky enough to get forever with a great man.

She drew in a deep breath, trying to commit to memory how he smelled. If only she could memorize every inch, take to heart all of him. But she didn't have time. Sepher was out there, watching like a snake ready to strike.

"The police are watching the street. You'll be safe today. We'll figure out something. I'm sure your brother will be caught soon. I hate that I have to go to work."

"It's okay. Go, I'll be fine. I need to check in with work, too."

His lips brushed over hers, and she almost lost her resolve to walk away. This man was too good for her. She'd known it the moment she'd seen him.

After Ethan drove away, Sunshine packed her belongings and sat at the table to write him a letter. The first two attempts, she tossed in the trash. The third one, she gritted her teeth and just spit out the truth. The words had to be said. She couldn't let Ethan get hurt because she was in his life.

It was noon before she took her bags out to her car and stuffed them into the trunk. She didn't want to leave, but she didn't see any other way out of this. Sepher would keep coming after her, and Sunshine couldn't allow Ethan to get hurt.

She headed over to the police car after she slammed her trunk shut. "Hey, I'm going to be staying at my apartment."

The officer narrowed his eyes and gave her a nod. "I'll follow behind. Are you sure that's what you want to do?"

She shrugged, then nodded, not trusting her voice. No, this wasn't what she wanted, but it was what she had to do.

Tears slowly slipped down her cheeks as she

drove the few miles to her place. Leaving Ethan hurt worse than anything she'd ever done in her life. She prayed he could find someone else to make him happy. She wished it could be her with him, but there was no way she would put him through the pain of being with her while Sepher was out there.

CHAPTER 13

Ethan panicked when he didn't see Sunshine's car in the driveway or the cop car on the street. Shit. Maybe she'd gone to the doctor. He'd asked Sunshine to call if she ended up heading to the doctor's office, but maybe she'd forgotten.

He rushed inside, noticing the difference right off. The place didn't smell the same. It seemed like his house had been empty for hours. His stomach twisted as he stepped into the kitchen and saw the white envelope propped up on the table with his name scrawled across the front.

"Mother fucker," he snarled as he marched to the table, ripping the letter from its place, knocking over the saltshaker.

The words blurred, and he had to start over

again. A roar set up in his head then came out as he tossed the letter to the ground. Anger and pain boiled. He almost flipped his table, but he drew in a slow breath then blew it out before bending to pick up the letter.

There had to be a clue in here about how she really felt. He read the first line once, then twice, then a third time, noting how she phrased the words. *I can't stay. Sepher ruins everything, and I can't have him ruin you.* She didn't say she didn't want to stay, but she couldn't. That had to be something. He looked at the rest of the letter, picking apart the words. Nowhere in the letter did she say she didn't love him. Instead, at one point, she said *I need you to be safe. I need to protect you from him. I can't be happy if you're injured.*

"Son of a bitch. She left because of that asswipe." Ethan resisted the urge to rip up the note. Instead he smoothed the paper, laying it on the table before heading to his room. He changed clothes then grabbed a quick sandwich. It wasn't what he wanted to eat, but he needed to head over to her place and convince her to come home. This was her home, not some apartment where she would hide from Sepher.

Minx was about to head out when someone knocked at his front door. He yanked it open, not bothering to hide the rage and anger. His chest heaved, and he may have looked frightening. Based on how Jenna took a step back, he knew he did.

"Minx," Vine called from behind Jenna. "What is wrong?"

"Where is Sunshine?" Jenna asked in a soft, comforting voice.

It did little to calm the raging beast inside him. He thought of pounding his chest and roaring to the heavens. Vine would be pissed if he scared Jenna more. The woman may be tough, but she was pregnant with Vine's baby. The man was an overprotective alpha and wouldn't hold back if he thought anyone, even his brothers, upset his woman.

"Hey, where is she?" Vine asked.

"Gone." The word came out as a wail. He sounded pathetic. Maybe he was pathetic. He hadn't kept her safe. They'd looked for Sepher, but he'd found a way to go deep enough even Tex couldn't find him.

Now Sunshine was gone. It was exactly what Sepher wanted for Sunshine. He didn't want her happy, and she'd been happy here, right?

"What do you mean gone?" Vine asked.

"I came home and found the note on the table. All her stuff is gone. She's gone."

"Let me go talk to her," Jenna said.

Both he and Vine turned to stare at Jenna. She'd put on some weight with this pregnancy, but it made her look better, almost like she could claim to be some mother earth goddess if she wanted to. Maybe a woman who could be incredibly calm and was knowledgeable, kind-hearted, but a badass when needed was who Sunshine needed to talk to.

"I love her." His words made his knees shake. It was the truth. He'd fallen in love with Sunshine, and he wanted her. He needed her to understand they could take care of Sepher, that she would be safe.

"I'm sure she knows that, and that's why she left."

"What?" Vine asked.

Jenna chuckled. "She will do anything to protect those she loves. She doesn't want you hurt. You were hurt by Sepher, so in her mind, that probably means she feels that she hurt you."

"I hate that guy," Minx said.

Jenna chuckled. "I'm sure Sunshine hates him, too."

Vine was on his phone scrolling through something. "Rawlins says the cops have an idea where Sepher is. They are moving on him later tonight."

"Let's go to her place." He rambled off the address

and turned to head out. Jenna's hand on his arm stopped him. He didn't shrug off her touch like he would have if it had been one of the guys.

"Let me speak to her first." Jenna's voice held a tenor that was pure steel. Vine's woman was one tough cookie.

Anger whipped through him, but he nodded, not trusting his words. He wanted to be the one to assure Sunshine everything would be okay, but he knew he would probably ruin it. He would command her to come home, and she would tell him to piss off. He needed Sunshine in his life and prayed it wasn't too late for them.

CHAPTER 14

Sunshine sat facing the door, wishing she'd gone to the gun shop and bought something for protection but knowing Sepher held some weird power over her, and if she had a gun, she might not be able to pull the trigger. She hated Sepher with everything she had, but he still had power to abuse her.

Maybe it was the fear he induced. He knew exactly what buttons to push to make her bend to his will. He knew how to get to her. Knew how to slip in under her defenses and force her to do his bidding.

The office she worked for had been great, understanding that she'd been kidnapped and wasn't just blowing off work for the fun of it. She was taking the rest of the week off then coming in the next week. She hadn't told them everything, not about Sepher getting away. They didn't need to know her brother was still out there and might attack at any moment.

She closed her eyes, wishing the words he said would go away. If he'd tied her up and beat her, raped her, she could have easily turned that anger on him. Instead, he held her and stroked her hair, telling her how much he loved her as he used stories from their childhood to guilt her into not rebelling against him.

She tried to get away once, and that's how Minx had found her. Tears streamed down her face. She missed Minx. He was perfect for her. Too bad she was a tragedy and the last thing he needed.

A knock sounded at her door, and she jumped. She must have drifted off at some point and hadn't heard anyone coming down the hall. The knock sounded again, and fear twisted higher, making it hard to breathe.

She stood, almost groaning as her muscles protested the movement. She'd been holding herself stiff since escaping Sepher, and now she was feeling the effects. If this was Sepher, she didn't know what she would do. But Sepher wouldn't bother with knocking. He would break in like usual.

"Sunshine, it's Jenna."

Her voice made Sunshine pick up the pace. She pulled the door open without checking the peephole, glad that it really was Jenna and that she was alone. The look on her face told Sunshine that she wasn't here just as a friendly visit. Jenna had seen Ethan. Her shoulders sank, and she closed her eyes, trying to fight the tears threatening to spill.

"He isn't going to give up on you," Jenna said as she wrapped her arms tight around Sunshine's back, holding her close as they both shed tears.

The door shut behind them, and Sunshine heard the lock turn, so she knew they were safe. She needed that safety. A shudder ripped through her, and Jenna held her tighter.

"He loves you," Jenna said.

Pain sliced through her. "I'm bad for him."

"He can take care of himself."

"Sepher almost killed him."

Jenna pushed her to arm's length. "Do you care for him?"

Sunshine tried to lie, but the words died on her tongue. She couldn't tell Jenna that she hated Ethan. If she had more strength, maybe she could convince Jenna she hated Ethan. She could get Jenna to tell Ethan she wanted him to leave. Instead, she closed her eyes and cried harder.

Jenna led her over to the couch and made her sit while she fixed tea and brought over a plate of cookies along with the mug of tea.

"Eat."

Sunshine sniffed, then took a sip of tea and grabbed a cookie, thankful someone had told her what to do. Maybe that's why Sepher burrowed his way in so easily. She did better when there was someone telling her what to do. If she were truthful, she would admit that she liked a little pain. Sepher knew her so well he knew exactly how to make her respond. It sickened her to think he could play her so well.

"Why did you leave Ethan?"

Jenna's question hurt. She didn't want to think of leaving Ethan. She was protecting him, not leaving him. But how could she make Jenna understand?

"I can't have Sepher hurt him."

"Honey, he's a Navy SEAL. He knows Sepher is out there now, and the man won't be able to get the drop on him again."

Sunshine shook her head. "I can't live with myself if he gets hurt again. I can't do it."

"He needs you."

Sunshine closed her eyes as pain filled her chest.

"He only thinks he does. Someone else will be better for him."

Jenna handed her another cookie when she opened her eyes. "You only think that now because you're upset. You two belong together. But I'm not going to force the issue. You need to come to that conclusion on your own."

Sunshine narrowed her gaze as she sipped more tea. Was Jenna trying to use reverse psychology on her? She longed for Ethan's arms but knew she would ruin his life. She couldn't hold anything together if Sepher hurt Ethan again. Her brother was bad news, and she had little doubt that he would ruin everything for her if given another chance.

"Listen," Jenna said as she sat forward and held Sunshine's gaze. "I know you're hurting, and it may seem like you'll never be free, but you will. You're going to have a great life, and I think you should give Ethan another chance. It doesn't have to be today or even this month, but don't cut him off. Give him a way to contact you and keep in touch. You two can build something amazing together."

Sunshine knew Jenna was right. They were great. Maybe they'd moved way too fast, and when the bad stuff happened, it was too easy to run because they didn't have as solid of a foundation as they needed.

Sunshine chewed on her lower lip. “I don’t know.”

“You care about Ethan.”

Sunshine closed her eyes and shook her head. “I can’t. He’s too good for me. I’ll only destroy him in the end. Sepher had this power over me, and I can’t let him hurt Ethan.”

“You do care about Ethan, deeply. Sepher will get caught, and he won’t bug you anymore. He’s about to be a thing of the past. Don’t lose your connection with Ethan. Just slow down.”

Jenna’s words made sense, but she didn’t know if she could do this. She’d messed up so much already. Would Ethan even want her?

“Hey, how about you and I—”

Shouting outside her apartment cut them off. There was banging and more shouting. Jenna stood and moved between her and the door. Sunshine couldn’t allow Jenna to get hurt, so she moved in front of her.

“You have your baby to think of. If someone is coming for me, I’ll deal with it.”

“You really are a good person, Sunshine. Give Ethan a chance.”

Fast knocking on her door drew her over. She checked the peephole and saw Vine. Without hesitation, she tugged the door open. Her gaze fell on Ethan holding Sepher down. Two police officers were coming up the hall fast.

Sunshine's eyes shot toward Ethan and a shiver skated over her nerves. The only reason she didn't drop to her knees was Jenna was there to hold her up.

"It's going to be okay," Jenna said.

Sepher looked up at her, his gaze pleading. "Tell them to let me go. Tell them to stop." Sepher's voice rose in pitch as he screamed at her. By the time the cops slapped the cuffs on him, he was yelling obscenities at her, telling her she would pay for letting the cops take him away.

"We'll need you all to come to the station to make a statement in the morning." The arresting officer had sat in front of her apartment yesterday and they'd talked. She'd told him about her fears, and he said he would make sure other officers took this seriously. Now he looked up at her, his gaze serious. "Miss Stephenson, he shouldn't get bail, but you never know. Your information will be entered into the courts' system, and you'll be contacted with any change in his status."

"Thank you." Sunshine shook the officer's hand

then watched him walk away, forcing Sepher in front of him.

Jenna stepped out of her apartment and Vine pulled her into a hug. She wanted to be with Ethan, but the threat of Sepher being out there was too much. Could she trust the police to keep him locked up?

Vine stepped away and then Ethan met her gaze. She flinched at the anger shining in his eyes. She was to blame, just like usual. She wanted to tell him to forget her, but the words stuck in her throat.

Ethan moved closer, his gaze holding hers. She wanted to back away, but she didn't move. The pull to be with him was too much.

"You shouldn't have left."

Her throat dried out too much to talk. She couldn't look away from Ethan. She wanted him back but knew she wouldn't be free to love him until Sepher really was gone forever.

Ethan took another step closer. She should turn around and slam the door. Keeping him safe was more important than her desire. "I get that you wanted to protect me, but this isn't the way."

Panic buzzed through her brain. How could she explain everything to Ethan—to herself? She gulped in a breath.

"I'm not giving up on you. You can sleep here, live here, but I'm not leaving you alone. I'll be around, calling you, texting you. We're good together, and you know it."

Frozen in place, she stared up at him. He hadn't turned away from her. He knew everything Sepher had done to her, and he wasn't walking away. A shiver snaked through her, and Ethan reached out, placing his hand on her shoulder, steadying her.

"I'll call you tomorrow. Get a good night's sleep." Ethan leaned in and brushed his lips over her cheek before he turned and left.

Jenna moved in for a hug and squeezed her tight. "He's a good man."

With that, they were gone. Sunshine closed and locked the door, leaning against the solid wood for support. Ethan hadn't forced her to come with him, and he also hadn't turned away from her. Maybe they could have something after all. But it would take work on her part. She was messed up from Sepher. Could she have happiness, or was she destined to be alone forever?

CHAPTER 15

Walking away from Sunshine last night had been the hardest thing he'd ever done. He sent her a text this morning, telling her he cared about her, and he hoped she had a good day.

He loved being a SEAL, but today all he wanted to do was go to Sunshine and make sure she was okay. He didn't have that luxury as work demanded he be on base. Some days he wished he didn't love the military so much. Being a civilian would be easier.

About an hour after they arrived at base, they were called into the conference room. Both his team and Mustang's team were in the room, and everyone seemed serious. This wasn't just them getting together to discuss a situation. One of their teams would be going out today.

He met Vine's hard gaze and knew it would be them. Vine must have received some intel earlier, and he knew they would be called up to step in and take care of business. Physically, Minx was ready. Emotionally, he wanted to see Sunshine before they left. He would be lucky to get a text off to her.

"Okay, folks," Captain Ashford said as he stepped to the front of the room. "Japan is asking for help. There's a situation off the coast. A group of pirates was able to take over a ship. They are asking for demands. If those demands aren't met, they are threatening to bomb Tokyo. Based on what we know about this group, the threat is credible. Mustang's team will be here for support. We have teams in Coronado looking over the situation. Vine, your team is up. We need you on the plane in twenty minutes. We know that doesn't give you much time. Your team is dismissed. Everyone else, send your condolences if you have plans for the next few days and get ready to settle in."

Ethan headed to the spot he'd stored his phone before walking into the conference room. He was texting Sunshine in seconds. His phone pinged him back, and he smiled as he read the text from her.

Be careful!

She still cared. They could work through the rest of the crap later, but for now, he would be satisfied with the idea that she cared about him.

They were in the air and on their way to Japan. Vine had them going through the files, looking at every angle. They would need to sneak onto the ship in the dark. By the time they landed in Japan, the sun would be up. There had been two attempts to get onto the ship, and both of them had failed. Japan had lost four men from their special defense force in the attempts to take back the ship. Now the stakes were even higher. Their attempts at raiding the ship had filed like their diplomacy had failed. Now the terrorists were preparing to bomb Tokyo in two days' time if they didn't meet their demands. Millions would die.

"This is a total shit show," Quirk said.

"We have to find a way in," Legs said.

"We have the brightest military minds working on this. We'll figure it out and get in," Vine said.

"I don't like this." Astro shook his head as he stared at the file.

"None of us do. They have all the power, and we're at a huge disadvantage, which is exactly where we shine," Wig said. "Think about it. We're the underdogs, and the last thing you want is a SEAL team going in as the underdogs. We'll figure it out, not because we're the smartest or the best, but because we don't give up."

Vine moved to stand behind Wig. "Good point. Get some rest, and we'll go at this when we have two hours left on the flight. We'll have some time for sleep before we go in, but not much. Recharge your batteries now. I need you all at one hundred fifty percent when we go in."

Minx sat back and closed his eyes, thinking about the ship and what they had to do. The rescue would be complex. The Japanese team that went in was good, but the SEALs were better. Now it was time to get to work to prove they had what it took to take down the worst terrorist in the world.

Once they landed, they took a few minutes to freshen up and grab what would probably be their last hot meal before they began their mission.

"You doing okay?" Quirk asked as he settled beside Minx.

"I'm great."

"That's good."

They ate in silence as they waited for Vine to give them instructions to move on. Once the sun started to get low, they would be on a tight schedule.

Anticipation wound through him as the minutes ticked by. This mission would be complex but so freaking fun. Maybe it would be fun because it was so complex.

When the sun had disappeared, they set off in black rafts heading a few miles out to sea. They had to drop into the water fairly far from the ship which meant they would be swimming underwater to avoid the patrols the terrorists had set up.

Once they found the ship, they had to climb up the side of the boat without being detected. That was the hardest part. Going up unseen would be the trick. If everything else went well, they would still have to get onto the ship unseen.

The atmosphere was tense as they slipped into the water. Minx was in the middle of the group, but they weren't staying together for long. They needed to be small targets, something that wouldn't be picked up on radar. Swimming through the inky black water was disorienting in a way. The moonless sky revealed nothing above, and the dark water hid everything below. He felt the water move when he came close to a big fish, or maybe it was a shark or a whale. He didn't know what he was swimming next to, but that didn't matter. He had his knife at the ready, he knew how to escape an attack, and he was prepared for anything unless the terrorists dropped a depth charge. Then they would all be screwed.

SEALs were usually too quiet to draw attention when they were in the water. Moving undetected in the ocean was their specialty. They'd learned to be like marine animals and the name SEALs fit how comfortable they were in the water. This mission should be their sweet spot.

He'd been in the water about an hour and was getting close to the ship. They'd used the tide and water patterns so they were going with the flow and could expend less energy.

Minx made it to the area of the ship, decreased his depth, and found the bottom of the ship. He kept the panic at bay as something touched his arm. He moved toward the object instead of away and found Quirk. They were working as quietly as possible to avoid any noise being picked up by microphones the terrorists could have dropped. One wrong move and the sound would reverberate through the ship.

After a few more minutes, the rest of the group found them. He moved with Quirk to the port side of the ship at the rear and started their climb to the top. Luck was with them, and no one spotted any of the SEALs.

Once onboard, Minx made his way to the engine

room. Vine was taking over the bridge, and Quirk and Wig were heading forward to take down the men manning any guns. That left Legs and Astro to take care of any rogue agents.

They'd made it this far, which was much better than any other group so far. When he was on the deck above the engine room, he heard someone in the hall outside the stairwell. He moved fast, knocking them out. They went down in a heap. He pulled them into a room and bound them with zip ties, making sure to take away all of the guy's weapons. He dumped the weapons in a storage closet and closed the door, hiding them from view.

He entered the engine room, which was massive, and slowly worked his way clockwise around the area, clearing each section. The engine room was three decks high, and he had to clear each one. He found one guy on the third floor hiding in the back. The dude tried to fight him, but Minx took him out quickly, binding his wrists and legs before tugging him out of the way so he couldn't damage any of the engine equipment if he came to.

Minx informed the rest of the group he was done with his tasks and headed up top. He came out on the open-air deck and was ready to head up to the bridge when someone hit him from behind.

He went down on one knee then turned, finding the barrel of a gun pointed at his head. There was no time to react. An image of Sunshine flashed in his mind. He would never get the chance to tell her he loved her again. This sucked.

CHAPTER 16

Worry ate at Sunshine. She turned on the news, but of course, there wasn't anything to give her a clue where Minx was headed. She wished she knew, but even if they were married, she wouldn't know where he was going. That wasn't information they were allowed to give out.

She thought about food, but she didn't want to get up to fix anything. Her phone rang about twenty minutes later, and she reached for it, answering before even looking at the caller ID.

"Hello?"

"Hey, it's Jenna. We're buying pizza and meeting at Ashley's place. Want to join us?"

She reached up and twisted a strand of hair. "Are you sure?"

"Yes. We all want to see you and we know you want to see little Oliver."

"But I'm not—"

"Just get your skinny butt over here."

"Hey, my butt isn't skinny."

"Whatever, lady, get over to Ashley's place now. We need to keep distracted, and Ashley needs some rest."

"Okay. I'll be there."

Sunshine headed out, then paused in the breezeway and went back to grab her stethoscope. It was fun for new moms to listen to the baby's heartbeats, and if she could get it positioned correctly, Jenna might be able to hear her baby's heartbeat.

She saw Jenna and Becky when she parked. They were carrying two boxes of pizza and seemed to be laughing. They were taking this better than she was. Sunshine felt like she was all nerves and worry.

"Hey, Sunshine, how are you doing?" Becky called out as she waved.

She liked these women. Maybe they could be good friends. Heck, if she was friends with these women, she would hear about Ethan and maybe see him. She couldn't take that if they weren't together. Maybe that was why she'd agreed to come over now.

She wanted Ethan, no question, but she knew she wasn't good enough for him.

They heard Oliver before they stepped into Ashley's place. Ashley looked like hell, and she probably felt like it, too.

"Thank God," Ashley said as she handed Oliver off to Sunshine. "I need a shower. I stink like puke and gunk."

Jenna grimaced. "God, I'm not going to survive this, am I?"

"You'll do fine," Becky said.

"I feel guilty that I didn't come over earlier," Jenna said.

"Don't." Ashley had snuck back into the main room with only a towel wrapped around her. "I still need to shower. I just wanted to say thank you for coming over. I swear I'll be back out here in a few minutes. At least Oliver is sleeping now." Ashley rolled her eyes.

Sunshine wanted to laugh but held it in for fear of waking the baby. It was obvious Ashley was having a hard time with her little one. She'd learned from being a nurse that babies did what babies did. Some things you could influence, but babies were just trying to adjust to the world around them. Everything they'd known had been taken away, and now the cold, harsh world was a reality they hadn't been prepared for with all the darkness they'd been in for months.

"Are you a baby whisperer?" Jenna asked.

Sunshine did laugh this time. "No. It's like a car or computer that is acting up, and as soon as you take it to get fixed, everything is okay. Oliver probably smells that I'm in the medical profession and is trying to make her mom look bad."

Jenna and Becky chuckled as they led the way to the kitchen. Sunshine took a set at the table and pointed to the sausage pizza. "A slice of that."

"Sure thing," Jenna said. She handed over the slice then frowned. "Can you eat with Oliver in your arms?"

"I have him tucked in well in my left arm. I'll lean over far and eat on the right side. It will be fine. You'll have a chance to hold him after you eat."

"Dang straight, I'm holding that baby. He's so cute." Jenna grabbed two slices of pizza and started wolfing them down.

Jenna and Becky were almost done with their two slices when a showered, and much calmer-looking Ashley stepped back into the room.

"I can't believe he is still sleeping in your arms." Ashley grabbed a slice of pizza and some water. "I swear when Robert leaves in the morning, he turns into a totally different baby."

"He's just learning his environment."

"I think he has it out for me," Ashley said.

Sunshine chuckled. "I'm sure it feels that way. Babies can be difficult. He seems very healthy."

"He is a chunk. I'm happy with his weight gain and eating, but he doesn't like sleeping during the day at all."

"So he is sleeping at night?" Sunshine asked.

"So far, so good," Ashley said. "I mean, it's not eight hours sleep, but I get four hours then three after I feed him. I'm happy with that."

"I'm going to need support when the baby comes," Jenna said.

"You'll be great," Ashley said around a mouthful of pizza. "I swear I thought I would be okay, but nothing in my life has prepared me for this."

They all laughed, and then Jenna washed her hands and waved at Sunshine. "I need to hold him."

Sunshine stood and moved to Jenna, who was sitting in a rocker in the den. "Here you go." She handed off Oliver to Jenna, who looked like she was in heaven. "Just think, in just a short while, you'll have your own little one." Sunshine grabbed another slice of pizza and sat next to Ashley.

"So, how are you doing?" Ashley asked.

Sunshine shrugged. "I'm fine. We don't have to talk about my problems."

"Oh, please. I need some adult conversation. I don't remember how adults sound."

Sunshine winced, knowing telling these women everything would open her up to their scrutiny. "I hate that my brother ruins everything."

No one said anything. They were watching her, but not with judgment. She'd never told anyone the full story, and she'd told them. Heat rushed over her.

"I'm so embarrassed."

Ashley moved fast and dropped to the ground beside Sunshine's chair. She rested her head in Sunshine's lap and looked up, smiling so sweetly it brought tears to Sunshine's eyes. "You have no reason to be embarrassed. You did nothing wrong."

Sunshine blew out a breath. "I just feel like I've come in and ruined Ethan's life."

"Trust me," Jenna said. "You haven't ruined his life. He wasn't happy before he met you. I mean, he did his SEAL thing, but there was a look in his eyes that seemed hollow. Ever since meeting you, that look has diminished."

Sunshine brushed her hand over Ashley's hair. "You all are so nice."

"We've been through a lot," Becky said. "We know what happened to you wasn't your fault."

"What if it was?"

"How do you mean?" Jenna asked.

"Sepher blames me. Said I tempted him."

Jenna narrowed her eyes. "How old were you?"

Sunshine shrugged. "Young. It was before I turned seven when he first started."

"Oh, honey, seven-year-olds are absolutely unable to be tempting at that age. And if someone is tempted by a seven-year-old, that's on them. They know to say no. He was older by how much?"

"Sepher was fourteen when I was seven."

"Sweetie," Ashley said as she stroked Sunshine's hand then moved to sit beside her. "Fourteen is young, but he was old enough to know he shouldn't touch you. You were not at fault. Sepher can tell you over and over again it was your fault, but it wasn't."

"I just can't help but think I'm to blame because..." Sunshine hid her face as embarrassment washed over her. "It felt good sometimes."

Becky shook her head. "Sex does feel good sometimes, even when you don't want it to. When I was trapped in that brothel, some of the men knew how to make women feel good. They weren't all assholes, and yes, I had orgasms. But I wasn't there by my own will. Your brother didn't give you a choice. He did what he wanted to do, and you didn't have a say."

Sunshine shook her head. "I felt like a prisoner. I was so depressed. Now that he found me here in Hawaii, I feel like I'll never escape him. He knows where Ethan lives. If he ever gets out, he'll kill Ethan."

Jenna stood and placed Oliver in a bassinet across the room from them. All of them smiled as he settled in for a nap.

Ashley shook her head. "You all are miracle workers. I haven't been able to get him down that easily."

"It's because you are his mom," Sunshine said.

Ashley's eyes narrowed. "What do you mean?"

"He has smelled you his whole life. He knows that you're attached to him. When he smells you, and then you put him down, your smell goes away. He just wants to be close," Sunshine said. "Eventually, he'll get used to other smells, but the scent of you was all up in his nose. He wants that close at all times."

"It's so weird," Ashley said.

"What?" they all asked.

"That we carry those little creatures in our bodies

then they are humans. It's just weird. Like all of us were that small."

Becky chuckled. "You're getting philosophical now."

"I think about life cycles, okay. I spent a lot of time in the ocean, and I've seen baby whales and sharks and all other types of little swimmers, and it's just weird how some animals are in eggs just lying around on the ground or floating through the ocean and then mammals are inside the mother."

Jenna patted Ashley on the shoulder as she headed into the kitchen. "You need some sleep. Why don't I stay over here and get up with Oliver?"

"I'm still breastfeeding. I'll have to wake up, anyway."

"Sure, but if he gets upset and won't go back to sleep after you've fed him, I can take him to a different room, and hopefully, you can sleep."

Ashley shrugged. "It's your call. I do need more sleep."

"Do you think Sepher will get bail?" Becky asked.

Sunshine shook her head. "The judge said no for now. He's a flight risk, and he's dangerous. So no, they want to keep him locked up. I don't know how long that will last, but for now, he's in jail."

Becky draped an arm over Sunshine's shoulder. "Do you want to stay at my place tonight?"

Sunshine thought about saying no straight away but shrugged. "I mean, I guess. You don't mind?"

"No way. I'd love to have you. When do you go back to work?"

"On Monday."

"That will give us some time together. And we can come over tomorrow morning and help with Oliver, so these two can maybe take a nap and get a shower? Does that sound okay?"

"Yes," Ashely said with a sigh. "I love him so much, but I'm so tired."

"It will get better," Sunshine said.

"When?" Ashley fell back against the couch cushions and closed her eyes as she laid her arm across her forehead.

They all giggled at her antics. Sunshine liked these women. They weren't fake or mean at all. She enjoyed their company and could see herself being friends with them for a long time. It was the teenage years she'd wanted but couldn't ever have, but this was better because they could drink wine on occasion.

"We'll help you get through the worst of it," Jenna said as she patted Ashley's shoulder.

A heavy sigh escaped Ashley's lips. "You all have jobs."

Jenna pulled Ashley into a hug. "Sure, but I'm leaving my job for at least two years. I'm not sure if I'm quitting this week or next, but I'm not working for a long time."

"That's nice," Becky said wistfully.

"We talked about it and decided we both wanted this. I know it will interrupt my life, but I was an agent for a long while, and I still have money set aside. I need a break and maybe this will be the break that makes everything better."

"I'm on leave for another four months," Ashley said. "I'm not sure how I'll leave him when I go back. I mean, I can do some of the stuff from home, but I'll still need someone to take care of him. I've contacted a few places, but I don't know."

"You'll figure it out," Jenna said.

Ashley shook her head. "You have a lot of confidence in me. I'm lost. I don't know what to do, and I have a little human depending on me, and it's too much. I can't even decide if I'm cooking dinner or just giving up and living on ramen and scrambled eggs."

Sunshine moved to Ashley and pulled her into a hug. "Hey, it's okay. Your hormones are out of whack, you just had a baby, and life is different now. You don't have to make all the decisions right at this moment. You can wait."

"But what if I wait too long and the daycare I want isn't available?" Panic filtered through Ashley's voice.

"Hey," Jenna said as she smoothed her hand down Ashley's back. "You know I'll have my baby before you go back, and I can watch him for a little while if you don't get the person you want to watch him."

Ashley shook her head. "That's too much to ask."

"No, it's not. I'm offering. You're not asking."

"What if you get overwhelmed?"

"I was thinking of hiring someone to come in for a few hours each afternoon."

Ashley narrowed her gaze. "You were?"

"Yes. Even if they're there for four hours, it will help. And you're not going back for another two months after I have the baby. So I'll be at home along with whoever I hire. It will be cool."

Ashley bit her lower lip as she stared at Jenna. Sunshine squeezed her shoulder before stepping back.

"You know, the both of you can probably work something out. It sounds like a good situation," Sunshine said.

Ashley blew out a breath. "We really didn't plan on this. So much for protection. I hate that it failed us. I sound ungrateful when I say that, don't I?"

"It's okay," Sunshine said.

"You are too nice," Ashley said.

"No, I've just seen a lot of women in Alabama and Louisianan go through postpartum depression, and they really think they are doing stuff wrong. They aren't abusing their baby, they care for their kids, but they have so much pressure on them to be perfect. You don't have to be perfect. Raising kids is hard. There's no reason for me to put extra stress on you. You're a good person and a good parent. You'll be fine, and your baby will be fine because you care."

Tears ran down Ashley's face. She leaned in and hugged Sunshine. "I'm glad I have all of you as friends."

They all agreed as they moved to the kitchen to chat while they put up the leftover pizza. Jenna and Becky cleaned the kitchen while Sunshine went to each bathroom, spraying cleaner into the sinks and showers before scrubbing the toilets.

Sunshine came back into the den and found Ashley quietly nursing Oliver. Ashley looked up, her smile wide. "Thank you. You didn't have to do that."

Sunshine's lips spread into a huge smile. "I know.

But now you don't have to clean them for a week or so."

Ashley looked down at Oliver, and her lips spread into a huge smile. "I hope your daddy is okay."

"Ugh," Jenna said as she flopped down on the couch beside Ashley. "I don't even want to think about what they are doing. I'm scared, but I know they'll be okay."

"Do you really think they will be?" Sunshine asked.

"Yeah. They're amazing. They'll be fine," Becky said.

Sunshine swallowed over the fear building inside. A weird feeling twisted through her. She didn't want to say anything or freak them out, but she had a bad feeling about the guys, specifically Ethan. She just hoped she was wrong.

CHAPTER 17

Minx swept his legs, jerking his right leg back, pulling the guy holding the rifle at his head to the ground. The gun went off. Luckily for Minx, the shot pinged off the ceiling a few yards away. Minx scrambled up, trying to get on top of the guy. He lost his hold and rolled to his back when the man shoved him. He wouldn't survive if he couldn't get this guy on his back.

Minx used his legs to gain an advantage, pushing up with his hips before rocking his chest up. He was able to push the guy off and climb onto the man's back. He slipped his arm around the dude's neck and squeezed.

The guy almost threw him off, but panic abated

as he squeezed harder, cutting off the man's air supply. He was about ready to let go when the guy pushed hard, almost knocking him away. The dude was big, strong, and knew how to fight. But Minx had the upper hand.

It took a long moment, but the man finally stopped struggling. Minx cuffed his arms and legs, then bound him to a rail, securing him in multiple places. He probably didn't need to use as many zip ties, but he figured this guy knew how to break free and would.

"Check in," Vine said over coms.

"Minx here, all is good. Found a few and took them out of commission. Was attacked on the open-air deck and took him down."

"Quirk and Wig are good," Quirk said.

"Legs and Astro checking in. We've disabled six men. I think we're in a good position."

"We need to check the whole ship. I'm calling in the Japanese defense force," Vine said. "I think they can retake this ship and count the terrorists as defeated."

"Sounds good," Minx said. "I'll keep checking on this level."

"I'll keep moving around with Astro," Legs said.

"Quirk and I will keep moving, checking as we go."

"Shit, this ship is huge," Astro said.

Minx chuckled as he moved to the starboard side. He was midship when he found a bomb with a countdown timer. It had eight minutes on it.

"Well, shit," Minx said.

"What?" Vine asked.

"Bomb with a timer. We have eight minutes. First open-air deck."

"Shit," Vine grumbled.

"I'll be there in a moment," Wig said.

"Jesus. This sucks. I'm coming," Vine said.

About two minutes later, Wig ran up and dropped to the ground next to the bomb. "Fuck. Six minutes. This is fucked."

Minx shined his light on the bomb, allowing Wig to check out the wiring. Vine arrived right after him, followed by Legs and Astro.

"I don't like this," Vine said.

"We can run up two decks and jump into the water. I think it would take us about a minute to get clear. So we have four minutes to get this taken care of," Legs said.

"Great. No pressure at all," Wig said.

Minx studied the bomb. He didn't know as much as Wig, but he could see they might have an out.

Wig glanced around and met Minx's gaze. "You good with helping me?"

He nodded. "Yes. I think I see an out."

Wig nodded. "I'm going to go over it with you."

"Sure." The pressure in Minx's head grew. He worried for a moment he wasn't on his game because of the concussion. But this wasn't because he'd been knocked around my Sunshine's brother, this pain was just pressure of finding a bomb and knowing they could all die in the next few minutes.

Wig started talking, detailing how he thought he could disarm the bomb. Minx nodded, agreeing with each move Wig wanted to make. He'd taken multiple classes in disarming, but Wig was the expert. He trusted his friend's plan.

"Sounds good," Minx said.

"Okay. Everyone back up."

"Shit, man, you just had a baby. Do you want me to do it?" Minx asked.

"No. I'm confident. Also, the baby gives me more reason to get home."

"Okay. Do it," Minx said.

Wig went to work on disabling the bomb. The seconds ticking past felt like tiny knives stabbing

Minx in the temple and neck. The tension ramped up. They had two minutes left. It would take one minute to get into the water and swim a little bit away, but they could still be hurt by the bomb. It had to end now.

Sweat slid down the side of Minx's face. He was about to tell Wig to abandon the bomb when the timer stopped ticking. They'd done it.

"Thank God," Wig breathed out.

"Yeah, man, I thought we were going to have to make a run for it."

Wig chuckled and stood then pulled Minx into a hug. The bomb was disarmed and they weren't dead. He closed his eyes, knowing it had been close this time. He needed to convince Sunshine they had to be together.

The Japanese military arrived, and the SEALs hopped aboard a helicopter and were flown to the base. Silence filled the chopper with each of them lost in their own thoughts.

Minx had fallen hard for Sunshine. She was his light, his air, and he didn't want to lose her. She meant the world to him, but his job was dangerous. The bomb wasn't the first one they'd faced, and it wouldn't be the last. This mission, the next, one of them years down the road may be the end for them, but he didn't want to give up. He wanted Sunshine with him. Now he just had to convince her that he was in this for the long haul. She might have issues, and her brother might be a psychotic jerk, but Minx wasn't going to give up. They deserved to have some happiness, even if it turned out to be short-lived.

CHAPTER 18

Sunshine visited Ashley on Sunday then after work on Monday and Tuesday. When she showed up on Wednesday at Ashley's place, she was surprised to find Robert answering the door.

"Oh, you're home. I just stopped by to help with the baby. But since—"

"Nonsense, come in. I'm not used to the little guy. I may be able to take out a squadron of enemy combatants, but he has me at a disadvantage."

Sunshine chuckled. "It's because you care."

"I do. I care so much about him. He's so darn cute. And he grew so much while I was gone. I also swear he doesn't remember me. He looked at me funny at first when I came home."

"Well, he is only weeks old. You were gone for a good part of him being alive."

"Ouch." Robert clutched his hands over his chest.

"Sorry. That was probably cruel. The good thing about babies is if you are good and kind to them when you're around, they'll love you."

They stepped into the kitchen, and Robert took Oliver from Ashley and settled at the kitchen table.

"Hey, Sunshine. It's good to see you."

"I see your helper is back," Sunshine said.

"He sure is. It's easier when he's here. He came home at around eleven last night and took over. I swear he's the best man on the planet," Ashley said.

"I'm glad you two are working together so well. It makes me happy to see my friends happy."

"So have you talked to Minx—Ethan?" Robert asked.

Sunshine shook her head. "No, not yet."

"He'll be around soon," Robert said.

Worry hit Sunshine. "Around? As in here?"

A knock sounded on the door, and Sunshine jumped. "Did he know I was here?"

Robert shook his head. "I asked him to dinner."

That still didn't answer Sunshine's question. She was forced to answer the door because Robert was busy with the baby and Ashley was cooking dinner. Sunshine straightened her shoulders before she pulled the door open. No amount of pulling herself together could prepare her for seeing Ethan. Her breath wheezed out as she tried to recover.

Ethan's lips curved into a smile, and he stepped in, crowding her in the front hall. "Hey, it's good to see you." Ethan moved fast, brushing his lips over her cheek before stepping all the way in and closing the door.

Sunshine's hand went to her cheek, rubbing the place where he'd kissed her. She felt like she was moving in slow motion as she stared after him.

"Hey, is that the little prince?" Ethan whispered as he bent and moved closer to Robert.

Sunshine watched as Ethan took Oliver from Robert, cooing to him. He let out a loud squawk then something like a laugh before making some cooing noise. Sunshine's heart squeezed hard. She wasn't prepared to see Ethan or watch him be so good with Oliver.

Ethan sat down and talked to Oliver for a long moment, letting him play with his fingers. When he looked up and met her gaze, it felt like a thousand pinpricks hit her all over. A shiver worked from her head to her toes.

"You look good." Ethan's voice was low and sexy. She couldn't help but move toward him.

"How was your trip—mission? I don't know what should I call it."

"Mission. I can't really talk about it, but we all came back alive and well, so I'd say it went well."

"I don't remember which day it was, but I felt like a heavy weight was on my chest at one point. Then it lifted and I knew you would be okay."

Ethan swallowed hard and looked down at Oliver. She swore she saw a haunting look in his eyes. She reached out and touched his shoulder, and the tightness around his eyes softened. Heat raced up her arm to her neck, and she pulled her hand back, but Ethan caught it and brought it to his lips.

"I missed you."

She swallowed, unsure what to say. No question, she missed him, too, but could she bring him back into her crazy with Sepher out there? What if her brother got out of jail? She didn't want Ethan to get hurt because of her.

Robert came in and grabbed Oliver from Ethan. "Sorry, I want my little guy back."

"I totally understand. He's addictive," Ethan said.

Sunshine had moved over to the window,

looking out at the yard. Ethan moved behind her, his hand resting on her shoulder.

"I can't," she whispered then glanced up, noticing his expression went tight again.

"Why?"

"You know why."

"No, I don't. Your brother is a dick. We know he's here, and right now, he's in jail."

"If he gets—"

"Do you want to live your life worried about the ifs, or do you want to live your life enjoying the people around you? Our time on earth is limited. If I go out on another mission in a month or two, or four years from now and I don't come back, will you be happy knowing you didn't give me the greatest gift of all, or would you rather look back on that time and know you gave me the best years of my life?"

His words twisted through her, making her ache inside. She would be devastated if Sepher killed Ethan. So many people had died around her, from the women who lived downstairs to Michael and who knows who else. Sepher wanted her, and no one could stand in his way. It would be that way forever. She would never have happiness, or...

Sunshine studied Ethan, taking in his dark eyes,

his dark beard that covered his jaw, his full lips that played havoc on her. He would be a wonderful man to spend the rest of her life with. But what if that life was cut short because she was in the picture?

"I would be devastated if Sepher killed you."

"Honey, so would I, but we can track him now. What are you going to do? Run again? That's no way to live."

She closed her eyes, knowing what Ethan said was right. It just hurt too much to think of Sepher winning.

The baby let out a piercing cry, and they both drew in a deep breath and glanced toward the kitchen where Robert and Ashley were taking care of Oliver.

"Listen, we can talk about this later. Just don't cut me off."

She turned back to Ethan and stared up into his eyes. He gave her hope which she hadn't had for a long time. Being with Ethan had been amazing, but they would have to do it different this time.

She gave him a short nod before she turned and headed to the kitchen. She took Oliver from Robert and rocked him while the guys set the table.

"He's a handful," Ashley said.

"I can hold him while you eat if he doesn't want to go down," Sunshine said.

Ashley frowned at her. "That's not fair."

"It totally is. I just want to sit and chat with you all. I don't mind waiting."

"Okay, if it's okay with you." Ashley came close and kissed her baby on the cheek before turning back to the stove.

Dinner was on the table in minutes, and they all sat around talking about what they had planned for later in the week. The guys wanted to go hiking.

"Do you think the baby can handle it?" Ashley asked.

"We'll go early and take an easy route. We'll have six guys to carry the baby. Vine went out and bought a baby carrier big enough for us guys to use. He figures we can trade off who carries the little tykes as we go on adventures."

Ashley nodded, but the far-off look in her eyes probably meant she didn't feel totally confident. Sunshine switched positions she was holding the baby and grabbed her glass for a sip of water.

"I'm sure you're nervous about taking the baby out," Sunshine said.

Ashley chuckled. "I am. But I know these guys would do anything for Oliver and me."

Robert reached for her hand. "It really will be an easy route. More like a walk, nothing big, just some time in nature, enjoying the island we live on. There's a path we do runs on that is flat but beautiful. We were talking about doing that."

After a moment, Ashley nodded. "Okay, it sounds good. Sunshine, you're going with us."

"Oh, I don't—"

"Please?" Ethan asked. "I'd really enjoy spending time with you."

Sunshine held her breath for a moment, and Oliver squawked. Everyone laughed, and Sunshine rolled her eyes then nodded. "Fine, I'll go."

"Good. I'll pick you up at seven on Saturday."

Ethan looked quite pleased with himself, and she guessed he should be. He'd gotten his way. And if she were being honest with herself, she didn't mind him having his way. She ached to be with him, but could she put away her fears? So much of her life had been dictated by doing things that wouldn't upset Sepher, or her running from Sepher. Could she choose to live for herself, picking pleasure over worry and fear?

CHAPTER 19

Minx hardly slept on Friday night. He couldn't wait to spend time with Sunshine. After coming back from Japan, he could tell she needed more time for them to get to know each other. She needed to learn to trust him. He was okay with it taking a few weeks, maybe months for her to get comfortable again with the idea they could be together and not worry about her brother attacking them. As long as they were moving forward, she could take as long as she needed.

The morning temperature started off pleasant, which was good since Oliver was going with them. They were surprised when Quirk insisted he be given the first chance to hold Oliver. The man was the least father-like guy in the group, but Oliver did something to him.

They'd gone about two miles when Oliver decided he needed to eat. There were benches in the shade, and Ashley settled there to feed the baby. Sunshine wandered down the path, and Minx followed.

"Hey," he said as he approached.

"Hey yourself."

"Did you have a good week at work?" He wanted to reach out and touch her, but he kept his hands to himself.

"It was okay. The district attorney called."

"What did he have to say?"

"Louisiana wants to extradite him. It looks like there was a woman I used to work with who went missing. She was found in a drainage ditch. They have video of her leaving work and being taken by Sepher."

"Oh shit. That's awful."

"Everywhere I go, he kills people. I couldn't stand it if—"

Ethan ran his fingers over her shoulder. "Hey, we'll keep you safe."

She shook her head. "I should do more to keep you all safe."

"He's in jail. If they extradite him to Louisiana, he won't be on any of these islands. We'll do better at keeping watch on him."

She closed her eyes, and he moved fast, pulling her into a hug. She tilted her head up as he looked down, and he couldn't pass up the opportunity. His lips found hers, and the kiss was magical. He felt like he'd never kissed anyone before her. She was sweet and special, and he never wanted to let her go.

When the kiss ended, he didn't move away. She clung to him, which was good. He would be crushed if she pushed away and told him never to kiss her again.

"You are a danger slut, aren't you?" Sunshine's words made him burst out laughing.

"Maybe," Minx said. He lowered, so his lips were right beside her ear, and whispered, "But I can be another type of slut with you if you'll let me."

"Oh God, Ethan. There are other people here."

He glanced around, seeing they were mostly alone. "They didn't hear. And if they did, they'd be happy for us. These guys want us to be happy."

Sunshine let go of him, and he thought she was going to step away. Instead, she grabbed the front of his shirt and pulled him down so their eyes were level.

"If Sepher comes after you, you kill him. Don't think for one minute I would be upset because he's my brother. Put a knife in his heart, or better a wooden stake, because there's no way someone as sick as him is human."

Her eyes burned hot as her words, causing his throat to tighten. When he spoke, emotions tinged his voice. "Babe, I won't let him win. If he escapes prison, I'll take him out, and no one, not the cops, not the FBI, no one will ever know it was me."

Sunshine seemed satisfied with his words and gave a sharp nod before walking away. He watched as she moved to Ashley and took the baby so Ashley could put herself back together after feeding the baby.

"She's full of fire," Legs said.

"She is."

"Want me to contact someone about her brother?"

Minx glanced at Legs, then shook his head. "Let's give the government time to get it right."

Legs nodded then walked off. Minx would do whatever was needed to keep Sunshine safe. He needed to pay a visit to Rawlins and maybe even Tex. Sepher was a blight on the earth. The jerk had killed one too many people and needed to be taken out. Maybe the harsh sentencing in Louisiana would do him in.

They started hiking again, and this time Vine took the baby. He looked like a natural carrying Oliver. Minx stole a glance at Sunshine, wondering how she would react if they were having a baby. He imagined that in five years going out for a hike would look a lot different than it did even today. They would have kids in tow, more women in the group, and he bet they'd be happy as clams. At least he hoped so. He was going to do what it took to keep Sunshine happy. That was a promise he planned on keeping.

CHAPTER 20

Spending the weekend with Ethan and his friends had been nice. On Monday and Tuesday, she worked late because of a conference the doctor was heading to on Thursday, and she didn't have a chance to see Ethan. By Wednesday night, she sat in her kitchen, wondering what the protocol was for contacting him. They'd been hot and heavy, then she'd cut him off, and now they were lukewarm. Should she call or just wait for him to contact her?

She really was going to wait, but she couldn't get him off her mind, and when she ran out to grab something from the grocery, she wound up in his neighborhood. He was out front by some miracle and waved her down.

It would be rude not to stop, so she pulled over.

He was right there, opening the door for her and helping her out of her car.

"Hey," Ethan said as he leaned in and brushed his lips over her cheek.

"I don't know why I'm here."

"I do," Ethan said.

Her eyebrows shot up as she stared at him. "Why?"

"Because you are deeply attracted to my body and wanted to see me naked."

Heat filled her face, and she moved to slap his chest, but he grabbed her hand and pulled her dangerously close.

"Come inside."

She bit her lower lip as a wicked mischievousness twisted through her. "I thought that's what I was supposed to say."

His eyes widened, and he gave no warning before his lips were on hers. He ended the kiss abruptly and grabbed her keys, locking her car before tugging her toward the house. Once inside, she held up her hand, blocking him.

He stopped short and dropped his hands. "Yes?"

"We're still using condoms. I was joking about the come inside."

His lips stretched into a wide smile. "I'm okay

with condoms as long as I'm with you. I'm totally okay. I just need you."

Sunshine gasped as he picked her up and slung her over his shoulder. The air was temporarily knocked from her lungs as the shock of his movement took her by surprise.

"Hey, put me down!" Sunshine yelled.

He moved fast, placing her feet on the ground. "Why?"

"You can't carry me. I'm too—"

"Don't say heavy. I can carry you, and I will."

He scooped her up again, and she shrieked then laughed as he carried her into the bedroom. He dropped her onto the bed then was on her, his lips kissing down her neck as his fingers worked on the buttons on her pants. She arched up into his touch, her need increasing with each second she was under him.

When he got her pants open, he sat up and tugged at her shirt, pulling it free. She helped him with her bra, and he sighed when his fingers found her nipple.

This was like coming home and finding that one thing that made you feel right after a long day. She pushed her pants lower then Ethan realized what she was doing and helped her with them.

He was up on his knees looking down at her, and she swore she could come just from the heat of his gaze. Then he dropped low and kissed her neck while his hands roved over her body. When his fingers brushed over the top of her slit, she came undone.

Ethan gasped as he cupped her and then deepened his kiss. After she finished riding the waves of her orgasm, he fumbled with his pants, finally getting them off. He tore off his shirt and grabbed for his nightstand.

A part of her wanted to tell him to forget the condom, but she wasn't ready for that level of commitment. She still had no idea how she was going to make a relationship with Ethan work. She didn't want her life to blowback on him. She needed to know he would be safe, but with Sepher still in this world, she had no way of knowing if any of them would be safe ever again.

Ethan rose up and placed a hand on her chest. "Are you really okay with this?"

Sunshine nodded. "Yes. I want you."

He moved into position and slid in, moaning as he filled her completely. They moved together, rocking against each other as they made love. She loved the feel of his body under her hands, loved how good he felt in her arms. They were good together.

His hands worked magic, taking her back to the top, leaving her wanting more. She wrapped her legs around him, not wanting to let him go.

His cock swelled even more, and he'd angled just right to brush against her clit. She couldn't take the sensation and came hard. Ethan slid in all the way and held still before shivering as he let out a low groan.

His body relaxed, and he let go a burst of air before peppering her face with kisses. She wasn't sure if she could recover or if she even wanted to. He made her feel things she had no idea she needed.

Ethan lowered, so his lips were next to her ear. "Don't leave me again." The whispered words wrapped around her heart and squeezed. "I need you."

A shiver slid down her spine. "I can't let him hurt you."

"I know. And I'm taking measures to ensure he won't hurt you."

She pushed at his shoulder, and he rose, pulling out at the same time. He took care of the condom then was back in bed with her, pulling her close.

"What does that mean?" Sunshine asked.

"Don't worry about it."

"Wait, why shouldn't I worry?"

He chuckled and kissed her cheek before turning to lay on his back. "There are certain things that are better if you didn't know. The cops can't get information from you if you don't know it."

Sunshine knew he was trying to protect her, and she guessed it made sense. If something happened to Sepher and she had information, she would do a shit job keeping it secret.

"Okay, you're right. I don't want to know certain things."

"We're not doing anything right now, just planning," Ethan said.

"That's good. Having a plan is good."

They lay together, her lazily brushing her fingers over his chest, him touching her arm and shoulder, then her hip. They were good together. No relationship had ever been this easy or this hard. Just the idea of Sepher hurting Ethan made her want to run to save him. But running wouldn't save him, not if Sepher got it in his mind he had to kill Ethan.

"You okay?" Ethan asked.

"Yes…no. I don't know. I've lived almost my whole life with this dark cloud over my head. I can't believe that it will be over soon. He'll be in prison for the rest of his life, and I'll never have to worry about him showing up on my front step. He won't ever track me and try to ruin my happiness. But it seems impossible. Like it won't really happen."

Ethan straddled her and placed his hands on either side of her head. "You're with the right group of people right now. We know how to track, trap, and take down bad guys. And if we do end up having to take him down, we'll make sure it looks like he did it to himself. We won't get in trouble for it. Hopefully, the courts will take care of him. But if they won't, or they can't, we'll be there to keep you safe."

"What would have happened if he'd been set free while you'd been overseas on a mission?"

Ethan dropped down beside her and pulled her close. "Rawlins or someone else I'm friends with would have disabled him. He wouldn't have gotten close enough to touch you."

She leaned back and stared at him. "Really?"

"Yes, really. He's being monitored. There's even someone inside the prison who is feeding us information. Your brother is exactly where we want him to be, and if he gets out, we'll know. He won't have the opportunity to get close to you again."

She let loose a long sigh. "It seems so out there I

can't even fathom being safe. I've spent years looking over my shoulder."

He kissed the side of her head and stood. "I'm starving. Come on, let me fix you something to eat."

She stood and grabbed a T-shirt from his closet, pulling it over her head. It hit just below her ass, and Ethan reached under the hem, pinching her cheeks as they headed to the kitchen.

"You're being very handsy," Sunshine said.

"Of course. I can't keep my hands off you. You're too beautiful, and I need you too much. I've been waiting days to get you into my arms again."

"Sorry I left."

Ethan came close and cupped her chin. "Listen, you were doing what you thought needed to be done to keep me safe. That you care about me that much to sacrifice something for my safety makes me feel good. But I'm safe. Your brother isn't going to get to me. I understand why you're afraid. He's killed a few people, maybe more than a few, but he's never come up against a guy like me. He's used to people who will roll over. I'll fight back and win."

Sunshine leaned in and rested her head on his chest, listening to his solid heartbeat. "Thank you."

"Babe, I care about you."

She looked up at him, her smile growing. "And I care very much about you."

"Good. Now we can get down to eating because I'm starving."

Sunshine stayed in the background as Ethan fixed their food. She thought he looked amazing, and that he wasn't afraid to cook and clean or take care of things like Sepher drew her even closer to him. She prayed they could make it through this. The last thing she ever wanted was her brother winning, and she felt with Ethan in her life, she just might finally have the upper hand.

CHAPTER 21

Sunshine didn't sleep at Ethan's house that night or the next. She kept going home for two weeks straight, wishing each time when she fell into her bed that she was with Ethan. She couldn't rush it this time. They both needed to take things slow and let their relationship develop over time.

Friday night, two weeks after she started sleeping with him again, she decided it was time to move in. She just needed to figure out a way to tell him.

They were taking care of Oliver while Robert and Ashley went out to dinner. Maybe after they got the baby to sleep, she would tell him she wanted to try living together. He'd brought it up more than once, and every time she told him to hold off. Now it was time.

She drove to Ethan's house then he drove them over to Ashley's. She opened the door, and based on the look on her friend's face, Sunshine thought Ashley was going to burst into tears of relief.

"Thank you so much for doing this. It's amazing that you're willing to help out."

"Of course, honey. We are happy to stay with this cutie for a few hours." Sunshine took Oliver from Robert and started chatting with the baby about his cute outfit.

Ethan gave both Robert and Ashley hugs before he came in and took Oliver, who immediately grabbed his beard and let out a baby-sized shriek. Oliver loved the guys and their beards. They all spent enough time with Oliver that he knew they were safe.

Once they were alone, Sunshine ordered pizza and picked up a little for Ashley. She cleaned the toilets and sinks, which is where Ethan found her.

"You know you don't have to do that, right?"

"I know. But if I can help her a little, I'm happy to do it. She's got other things to worry about."

"You are way too nice."

Sunshine chuckled and shook her head. "No, I'm just the right amount of nice. This is how friends should be."

"Well, I'm glad we're good enough friends to sit for them. I know we haven't discussed the future in a few days—"

Sunshine spoke, running over his words. "I want to move in with you."

Ethan gasped, and baby Oliver made a shocked noise. They both laughed then Oliver laughed, too.

"You do?" Ethan asked.

"Yeah. I miss sleeping with you."

Ethan looked at Oliver, then back at Sunshine. "Can we talk about this in front of the baby?"

Sunshine rolled her eyes. "He isn't going to understand us talking about sex, as long as we have a pleasant voice." Sunshine sang the last bit of her sentence then washed and dried her hands before taking Oliver. "You won't understand, will you, sweetie? We can talk about sex for hours, and you still wouldn't have any idea as long as we keep talking sweetly."

"God, that's disturbing."

"I mean, I wouldn't talk about it in front of a toddler, but Oliver is just forming connections in his brain. He won't remember the words or the topics. He'll only remember basic attitudes and tones. He's learning that we're safe, and we love him."

"I do love him. I love him more than I thought I could love a kid. It's weird."

Sunshine headed to the kitchen, and the doorbell rang. She turned, but Ethan was on the way to answer. Their pizza had arrived. They fed Oliver a bottle then set him in a baby chair as they ate their dinner.

"You know," Ethan said as he finished his second slice.

"What?" Sunshine asked.

"I wouldn't mind having a few kids with you."

Guilt filled Sunshine. "I still don't know if I can have kids. I've never asked a doctor."

"I get that's not a topic you want to talk to a stranger about. I'm here for you when you want to talk to a doctor. I'll go to the appointment with you and hold your hand."

"Wait, you'd go to the gynecologist with me?"

"Yeah, why not? This is important to your health. I don't expect you to do something so big on your own. I mean, it's not like you have a cold or a fever. This is something that could change the direction of your life. If you can't have kids, I want to be there to reassure you that we're going to be okay."

Sunshine stole a look at Oliver, and her heart squeezed. "Would we?"

"Of course. I wouldn't mind having kids, but if you can't give birth, that doesn't mean I'd leave. I like you for you. Having kids would be something extra we do together. It's not a make or break on our relationship."

Oliver started crying, and they both jumped up, trying to solve whatever problem he thought he had. His diaper was dirty, so that was probably the problem. After they got him changed, he looked like he wanted to sleep so Sunshine got him into warmer clothes and took him to Ashley and Robert's bedroom, where they had a rocking chair set up. Sunshine fed him half a bottle, and Oliver passed out. She placed him in the small crib set up next to the bed and flipped on the baby monitor.

Ethan had cleaned up the kitchen while she'd been busy with Oliver. When she stepped into the kitchen, he pulled her close and held her tight, swaying slowly as though they were dancing.

Worry filled Sunshine. "Do you think it's too early for me to move in with you?"

"Heck no. I think having you in my bed is the best thing I've heard this year."

Sunshine chuckled, and Ethan moved in for a kiss. His phone buzzed, and he sighed. He gave her a quick peck before pulling out his phone.

"Oh shit." Ethan's eyes widened, and his mouth dropped open.

"What?"

"They're taking Jenna in for an emergency C-section."

"Oh, crap."

His phone rang, and he answered. "Yeah."

Sunshine didn't know what to do. She worried something would happen to the baby or Jenna. Ethan grunted twice then ended the call.

"That was Ashley. They ran into Jenna and Vine outside of the restaurant. They were planning to go to another restaurant in the complex, but Jenna said she didn't feel good."

"Crap. I hope she's okay."

"God, Vine is going to be torn up."

"The baby is far enough along to survive. As long as Jenna is okay…" Her voice trailed off. She didn't want to think about Jenna not making it.

Ethan's forehead crinkled as worry filled his face. "What could it be?"

She shrugged. "I didn't specialize in maternal care. It could be anything. Hopefully, they'll be able to stop any trauma and keep her alive. That's the big thing, just keeping them alive through the birth."

Ethan ran his hand over his face, pulling hard on his beard. "Fuck."

The door opened, and Ashely hurried in. Sunshine met her in the hall and gave her a huge hug. Tears were shed, and they ended up being wrapped in Robert and Ethan's arms. Within ten minutes, the rest of the guys and Becky were there, all of them holding hands or hugging someone as they prayed Jenna and the baby made it.

Ethan's phone rang about twenty minutes after everyone showed up, and he answered, putting it on speaker.

"You're on speaker, Vine."

Vine cleared his throat, and everyone tried not to react. Becky was beside Sunshine and pulled her closer. Robert and Ashley had their arms wrapped around each other.

"It was a miracle," Vine choked out. "She wanted to go back to the house, but I drove us to the ER. They caught it just in time. Everyone is okay. This is our only baby, well, by birth. Jenna is still asleep, and they are going to keep her sedated for at least twenty-four hours, maybe longer. The baby is in the neo-natal ward tonight. I should be able to hold her tomorrow morning."

"I'll be there in a few minutes," Astro said.

"You don't—"

"I do, and I am coming up there. I'm going to bring you back to my place, and you can sleep in the guest room. We'll have you back at the hospital before the baby is awake or out of the neo-natal nursery."

"I feel so wasted," Vine said.

"Understandable. I'll be there in less than twenty minutes. Don't argue on this. I'm taking care of you tonight. Someone else will have tomorrow. We're going to help you get through this, brother, because you'd do the same for us."

Vine sniffed and grunted. They were a family. They'd all come from different areas of the country, they were basically alone in Hawaii with their parents, brothers, and sisters elsewhere, but this group of SEALs had come together and formed connections that were stronger than anything she'd ever known.

Astro and Becky took off, and the team made plans for helping out Jenna and Vine. Somehow they would make it all work. At ten, Ethan put his arm around her and led her out to his truck. They were silent on the way home. When they crawled into bed, she was glad she'd told Ethan she wanted to move in. There was no way she would have been able to leave him tonight. He seemed so broken up over what had happened. These men may be tough, but they also had hearts of gold.

Sunshine visited the hospital and held the baby as much as she could. She knew Jenna would want her there to show their baby love. They hadn't picked out a name yet, so everyone was calling her Sweet Baby. She thought it fit. She was small, but she wasn't too early. She would be able to go home before Jenna.

Before Sunshine headed home, she stopped by Jenna's room. Of course, Jenna wasn't awake yet, but the doctor was going to allow her to wake up today. Vine looked like he'd aged a few years in the space of the weekend. He flashed her a smile that looked more like a grimace when she stepped in, but his attention turned back to Jenna.

Everyone was worried about her. Sunshine had talked to one of the nurses she knew through work and had been assured Jenna was doing well.

When Jenna's eyes fluttered open, she thought Vine would pass out. He stayed upright, but tears streamed down his cheeks. It was good to see Jenna awake. It took her a moment to get more alert, but after about five minutes, she was ready to see her baby.

Sunshine went outside, not wanting to intrude on their moment when the nurse brought their baby into the room. Becky arrived along with Astro, Wig, and Legs. Sunshine was getting better with the nicknames and felt proud of herself. It was such a small thing in light of what was going on with Jenna, but it was also big. She was getting to know these people and they were family now.

"I'm glad she's awake," Wig said.

"She's tough," Becky said.

"She is." Legs nodded.

"I'm going to head home," Sunshine said.

"Hey," Astro said before she could leave.

"Yes?" she turned to face the guys, a little worried about what they would say.

"If you ever need anything, you know you can call on any of us, right? Minx is our brother, which makes you our sister. You are family."

Tears stung the back of her eyes, and she had to work to keep them from falling. "That's the nicest thing anyone has ever said to me."

"It's the truth. We care about you and will do anything to keep you safe. We're here for you," Legs said.

"Thank you. That means a lot to me." Sunshine left the hospital and headed home. She and Ethan were grabbing more of her clothes tonight. It felt right to finally be moving into his house.

Maybe they would experience issues, and they would surely fight, but they would make it through. She had little doubt about that now.

CHAPTER 22

Jenna and Vine's daughter, Lila, was two weeks old, and everyone was finally out of the hospital. Sunshine had taken the day off work to help out. Everyone was pitching in to make Jenna more comfortable and to help her keep the house in order.

The guys had gone over and cleaned the house from top to bottom the weekend after Jenna woke up. It was so clean, Sunshine wondered why the guys didn't start a cleaning service. She joked with Ethan about it a few times, and he said he might just do that after he retired.

It was nice to have a guy she could joke around with. They were getting along well. She thought they might decide to make their relationship even more permanent sooner rather than later.

"Hey, Lila, Auntie Sunshine is here. Funny thing about her name, it means the sun is shining outside and Sunshine means this wonderful woman, too" Jenna said to Lila.

"How are you doing?" Sunshine asked.

"Eh, I'm better. I was able to go to the bathroom alone today."

"Ah, progress. That's awesome."

"I'm itching to get up and move."

Sunshine chuckled. "Give it time. You'll be running circles around us soon."

"I have a woman coming tomorrow to interview."

"Wow, you are jumping on this."

"I can't do things like pick up the baby unless everything is right, and you can't take days off just to sit with me. I need help."

"You're right. You do need help. But we are here if you need us."

"Ashley will be here tomorrow and then Becky the next day. Hopefully, I'll have someone hired by then. Otherwise, a few of the other women said they would help."

"What happened was a huge deal. I'm glad Vine took you to the hospital."

"So am I, or little Lila wouldn't be with us. She's

fine, too. A few more minutes, and it would have been bad. She's small but mighty."

"She won't be small forever."

Sunshine took Lila and put her in a bouncy seat. She helped Jenna up so she could use the restroom and then started gathering food for lunch. She was glad she had time to help her friend. She couldn't imagine being so helpless and having no one. She saw it at work, and when she was in Alabama. There had been more patients in that area who weren't capable of daily care. Jenna wasn't used to being so dependent on others and it would take some getting used to. Sunshine just wanted to make sure she didn't push herself too hard.

"So you want tomato on your sandwich?"

"Yes, that sounds good. Cheese doesn't agree with Lila, though, so no cheese. What a bummer."

"She'll get used to it after a while. A few weeks or so without cheese isn't so big of a deal."

"No, it's not."

As Lila slept, they took their food outside, neither of them speaking much. When they finished, Sunshine took their plates inside then helped Jenna into the recliner. She put her feet up and dozed off while Sunshine ran around and did light cleaning.

When Lila woke, she helped Jenna get set up for a feeding, then went back to cleaning the kitchen.

"The guys did a great job cleaning," Sunshine said.

"It's the Navy in them. Those guys in training scared the crap out of them, and now they know how to clean."

"It's amazing. I think all men should go through that. Make them appreciate how to clean."

Jenna chuckled. "I like you. You're not pretentious at all."

"Thank you, I think."

"I didn't mean it like that. I just meant some women have to fill the air with the sound of their voice. I like just being with you."

"And I like being with you."

"You know, if we'd met under different circumstances, I'm not sure we would have been friends because neither of us would have talked to the other one."

Sunshine laughed, and so did Jenna. Lila popped off and stared up at her, a line developing between her eyebrows.

That made Jenna laugh even more. "She's not used to me laughing when I feed her."

"That's too funny. Her little face was scrunched up with worry."

Jenna got her latched back on, then glanced up. "She's a cutie. Thank you for everything you've done."

"I'm happy to help."

"Are you and Minx talking about having kids?"

Sunshine shrugged. "I still need to make an appointment with a doctor. I want to know if I can have kids, but I'm afraid to find out."

"I understand. It's hard knowing. But sometimes, the wait is worse than the knowing. Why don't you call and make an appointment today? My doctor is good. She'll be honest with you. When I came to, she was there and explained everything to me. I was upset I couldn't have more kids, but she was so good at explaining about risks and what would have happened if they had tried to save my uterus. It was sobering, but she was so kind about it. I was upset, but I wasn't devastated."

"Okay, I'll call."

Jenna gave her the number, and Sunshine placed the call, stating she needed to have an initial meeting with the doctor to discuss her reproductive organs. The nurse didn't ask any weird questions and set up the appointment for two days later.

"Dang, that was fast," Sunshine said.

"I'm glad you were able to get in so fast."

"Yeah, that's odd. They must have had a cancelation."

After leaving Jenna's place Sunshine headed home, arriving just as Ethan pulled in. He got out of his truck and held out his hand. "No hugging yet. I stink."

Sunshine laughed and moved toward him. "I don't—oh my God. What is that?"

"I told you I stank. I need to shower. Just trust me. You don't want to know."

"Do we need to roll the windows down on your truck?"

"Yeah. That wouldn't hurt."

Sunshine took his keys and rolled the windows down, almost gagging the whole time. She had no idea what had happened and wouldn't ask until after he showered. By the time she got inside, the washer was already running. The stink had followed him inside, and she opened the windows, getting a good cross breeze.

She found him in the bathroom as he stepped from the shower. "Do I still stink? I'm nose blind. I can't smell anything."

"Let me see. I don't think it totally burned out my

nose." She moved in close, taking a deep sniff. "It wouldn't hurt to soap up again."

Ethan got back into the shower and did another round of soap and shampoo. When he stepped out, he looked exhausted.

"Do I even want to know?"

Ethan shook his head. "Probably not. I love you. You're going to have to put up with shit like this from me from time to time. I swear I would have showered on base, but the water was out, and I didn't want to wait."

"I've got the windows open. I'll go spray some stuff in your truck."

Ethan's forehead wrinkled as he gave her a sad smile. "Thank you. You're awesome."

"You say that now. Just wait."

His chuckle warmed her heart. "Trust me, nothing you do will ever be as bad as what I just went through."

She took some air freshener out to his truck and sprayed the seats. She hoped it got rid of the stench. Already it was better, but the fresh air and sun could only do so much.

"So, how was your day?" Ethan stood in the center of the kitchen in this underwear looking absolutely adorable.

"I spent it with Lila and Jenna. So it was good. She made me make that appointment with the OB. I'm not sure if you can make it. It's at three on Thursday."

"I'll figure out a way to be there."

"If you can't—"

"I'll be there. And I'm glad you are doing this. We'll figure out what can and can't happen, and then we'll move on from there."

She placed her hand on his back and ran it up to his shoulder. He felt so good to her. It was more than just his muscles. Ethan was a nice person. "Thank you for being so understanding."

"Of course. I just want you to be happy. If you're happy, I'll be happy."

Sunshine chuckled. "You're easy."

Ethan barked out a laugh. "I'm so not, but I'm glad you think I am.

A sigh escaped her lips. "I'm glad Jenna survived."

"Vine would have been wrecked if she'd died. I've seen it in his eyes. When he thinks no one is paying attention, he gets this look in his eyes."

"Maybe he needs to talk to someone."

"I'm sure he does. I'll have a talk with him."

"Do you think he'll reject the idea?"

Ethan shrugged. "Probably. He's a tough goat.

Then again, we all are. It's not macho to need help with stuff like that. But you're right. He needs to talk to someone about it, even if it's me."

"Maybe you all can go do some man stuff this weekend, get him talking."

Ethan burst out laughing. "Man stuff. That's funny."

"You know what I mean. Go chop down a forest or go fishing. Something to get him talking."

"What about you?"

"We'll get together at Jenna's place and help her."

"That's not—"

"It'll be good for everyone. You all need to blow off some steam, and we'll get the chance to gossip without you being there."

Ethan's lips twisted to the side then he nodded. "I'll send a note to the guys, see if they want to do some man stuff."

"Good. Now then, how about some food?"

"I really didn't think I could eat after what happened today, but I think I can eat now."

Sunshine cooked eggs and heated sausages they'd cooked on Sunday. They ate outside, watching the birds swoop in for insects or something else in the back yard. After checking on his truck, they headed to bed early.

On Thursday, Ethan met her at the doctor's office. He looked nervous, and she felt like everything was riding on this appointment. She knew it wasn't. Ethan had said multiple times he didn't care if they had kids or not. She believed him, but still, a part of her worried.

She was put into a room but told not to change yet. The doctor wanted to talk first. Then they would determine what to do. She was glad Ethan was there when she told the doctor about her past. Somehow the doctor had no judgment in her eyes.

"I know you were young at the time. Is there any possibility your family forced you to get an abortion, and you don't remember it because they knocked you out?"

Sunshine blew out a breath. "I'm fairly certain my memories are correct, that I lost the baby naturally, but I don't know for sure."

"We can take a wait and see approach since your cycles seem normal. I'd hate to put you through unnecessary and invasive testing. If say in six months after you two actively start trying to conceive, you don't get pregnant, then we can hit it hard with tests. If you're having a normal period, and you believe your memories are correct, I would say you losing the baby was just because you were so young. Were you malnourished at that time?"

Sunshine blew out a breath. "I was painfully skinny. Our refrigerator and pantry were locked most of the time. I remember stealing food from a neighbor's house and getting caught. I got a severe beating for that. I think I lost the baby after that." Sunshine shook her head. "Funny, I just remembered that."

The doctor nodded but didn't react otherwise. There was no condemnation in her voice when she spoke. "Then I'd say your body was trying to protect you. It's awful what you went through, but I'm glad you survived."

"Thank you."

"Now then, let's do the routine screening, and we'll get you out of here."

Ethan left the room as Sunshine undressed and slipped on the gown. He came back in with the doctor and held her hand. The rest of the appointment was over quickly, and they left for home.

When he parked the car, Ethan reached over and held her hand. "Your childhood was horrific. I think you're the strongest person I know to have survived all that and still be around."

Sunshine shrugged. “It was what I was used to.”

He turned and hit her with a stare full of compassion. “My parents may have been strict, and I had to work hard in the yard each summer and do other chores, but I had free access to all the food I could eat. They never once told me I couldn’t eat. They may have said no to sweets, but there was always food. I can’t believe you…”

Ethan trailed off as tears slid down his cheeks. She moved to him and kissed his cheeks. “I survived.”

“You did. You’re amazing. I’m lucky to have you, and I don’t want to wait any longer to ask this.”

Sunshine narrowed her gaze and leaned back. “What?”

“Marry me. I know this isn’t the most romantic proposal—”

“Yes.” She cut him off, not giving him time to apologize for what he thought wasn’t romantic. “This is very romantic. I know you mean it. I can see it in your eyes. You want me.”

“I do. I really do. I want you forever. I want you to be my partner in everything. I can’t wait for life to be perfect. Your brother is out there. My life is at risk with every mission. There will always be something imperfect, but together we can smooth out those imperfections and make it right."

Sunshine pulled Ethan close and held him. "I love you. I can't wait to be your wife."

He pulled back and chuckled. "How long do you want to wait? Because I have no issue getting a license and asking someone to marry us at a park or at the chapel on base."

Sunshine bit her lower lip. "I don't want to wait long. I have no designs for doing a big wedding. There isn't anyone to invite over from the mainland. It will just be us, our little group. I'm more than happy with that."

"Do you want to talk it over with the women on Saturday while we do our man stuff, as you called it?"

Sunshine threw back her head and laughed. "God, I love you. And yes, I'll chat with the other women and see what we can come up with. It won't be long. We'll make sure it doesn't conflict with anything the military throws at you."

"That's a tall order. I could be called out right now."

"I know. So we'll be flexible. But know this, Ethan Olsen, I'm ready to marry you."

"Good. Let's go in and celebrate."

Sunshine couldn't remember a time she'd ever been so happy. Everything was coming together. They were both realistic enough to know life wouldn't be perfect, but they would take what life tossed at them and make it work.

CHAPTER 23

The weekend had turned out better than Minx had expected. Vine had agreed quickly that he needed to talk about everything. They'd planned on fishing, but in reality, they'd gone out on the boat, drank a few beers, and talked about how much fear Vine had held onto when Jenna had been so close to death. He'd felt hopeless, and that had knocked him for a loop.

The guys helped him talk through the pain and fear, coming out on the other side of the morning feeling better. Vine agreed to see a psychologist to talk through the rest of his pain. Now Minx felt like they could go out on a mission, and Vine wouldn't have any issues.

The women talked over the wedding and planned

for a small wedding the following Saturday. They would have a picnic after the ceremony, keeping it simple. On Monday, Minx learned they would have an overnight on Thursday, giving him most of the day off on Friday. Everything was working out for them.

On Thursday morning, he kissed Sunshine goodbye, making sure she had a list of people she could call if anything went south while they were overnighting on base. He felt confident nothing would go wrong.

Their day started slow, then they were helicoptered over to another island where they had a training mission they had to accomplish overnight. It sucked that he would be up all night, but the missions they went on didn't follow the daylight or their personal timelines. If they had to stay awake for seventy-two hours, then that's what they did.

As they were making their way through a dense jungle, Minx was hit with a load of worry. He didn't have time to wonder what was going on. He had to push the feelings away and concentrate on the task at hand. He would be home soon enough, and he had to trust Sunshine would be okay. She had to be okay because Minx needed her in his life.

CHAPTER 24

After work on Thursday, Sunshine picked up a salad on the way home, deciding she was going to watch some sappy romance movie while relaxing. She loved her work and was already planning on finding a permanent position in Hawaii. She wouldn't be leaving the area at the end of her contract, after all.

The salad was exactly what she wanted, and the movie left her crying in the middle and then so happy for the couple at the end that she cried again. When she turned off the TV, she locked up, making sure the house was secure.

She didn't need to worry because she hadn't received any notifications that Sepher would be let out or that he was being transported.

Sleep came easy, but she woke before the sun

rose. Panic swept through her. She pushed it away, thinking she was being ridiculous. She only needed to pee and there was nothing going on. She stumbled to the bathroom and sat on the toilet, still half-asleep, when the sound of metal scratching on metal woke her up the rest of the way.

Panic blazed through her as fear settled in. Someone was in their house. Sunshine quickly pulled up her panties, not flushing the toilet and making noise. Luckily, she'd not needed to turn on the light since both she and Ethan kept the house picked up enough, they wouldn't stumble over anything in the dark.

Fear pelted her as the metal-on-metal sound hit her again. Someone was breaking into the house.

Her hands shook and her stomach tightened. She didn't know what to do. Her phone was plugged in beside the bed where she slept. She had no way of getting to it unless she walked out into the bedroom. But what if the person breaking in was in the room? She had to do something.

Sunshine slowly made her way to the bedroom, fear making each step difficult. She felt like she might pass out at one point when the front door squeaked opened. She wished Ethan was here, but he wasn't.

Her phone lit up the room when she unplugged it, and she moved fast, slamming the device against her stomach. She didn't need the stranger seeing that she was up and moving around.

Sunshine turned and took one step, then another toward the bathroom. Could the person see her? What if they'd moved fast and were watching? A shiver almost made her drop her phone. She forced herself to calm. She would barricade herself in the bathroom and call for help.

She'd almost made it to the bathroom when the intruder spoke. "I've come for you."

A roar in her head blocked out all sound for a second. Sunshine shook so hard she almost dropped her phone. It was Sepher. He'd come back for her. She wouldn't live. Before he could race into the room, Sunshine slammed the bathroom door and locked it, praying it would keep him out until help arrived.

She pulled up Rawlins's number and texted 911 before calling the police emergency line. She just hoped help would arrive before Sepher got to her.

CHAPTER 25

Minx tossed his bag into the bed of his truck and opened the door. He called out to the rest of the guys before he slid into his truck. "I'll see you all tomorrow."

"It's wedding day. Are you ready?" Vine asked.

"So ready."

The guys had threatened to take him out for a bachelor's party, but he told them no, that their fun in the sand and the jungle had been enough for him. Besides, they'd partied enough over the years, and he didn't need a night of drinking. He just wanted to spend the night with Sunshine.

He was almost home when his phone rang. The traffic was low since it was so early, and he picked up his phone, checking the caller ID. It was Rawlins.

Minx had his Bluetooth in because he'd been listening to a podcast and clicked over to answer. "Hey, buddy, what's up?"

"I just got a 911 from your woman. Are you still on base?"

"Fuck," Minx sped up. "No, I'm about two blocks away. We finished early."

"Well, I think she's in a mess of trouble. A call went through dispatch just now. A woman is trapped in a bathroom with an intruder."

"Shit." Minx took the curve a little fast and almost ran up into his neighbor's yard. He corrected and raced to his house, slamming on the brakes before popping the truck into park and hopping out.

The front door was wide open, but he didn't see evidence of another vehicle. He prayed Sepher didn't have Sunshine.

Rawlins was still in his ear as he entered his house. "I just saw a note that they were transporting Sepher last night. Shit, he escaped. I think that's who is there."

"Dammit, if he has Sunshine, I'm going to kill him."

"I'm about five minutes away," Rawlins said. "I've sent a note to my friends at the PD. They know what's going on. Don't kill him if you don't have to."

Minx didn't reply as he slowly made his way through his house, searching for Sunshine and Sepher. He wasn't going to hold back. If he had to kill Sepher, then the guy would just have to die.

Sunshine's scream ripped through the house, chilling Minx to the bone. He raced into the bedroom and saw Sepher dragging Sunshine from the bathroom. The door was askew and looked like he'd broken it down.

Sepher had his back to Minx and Sunshine in a headlock. Minx couldn't shoot the bastard because he might miss and hit his woman. There wasn't any way he would put her at risk of being shot, so he would have to do hand-to-hand combat.

Minx silently moved closer, glad Sunshine was throwing a fit, screaming and yelling. That kept the attention off him, allowing him to move close and reach out, grabbing Sepher around the neck. Turnabout seemed fair play as he squeezed tight.

His surprise attack came at just the right moment, and Sunshine jerked away just as Minx pulled hard. Sepher lost hold of Sunshine. She was free. That's all that mattered.

Minx held on tight, blocking Sepher's airway with his hold. Sepher clawed at Minx's arm, but he didn't lighten up. If Sepher died, then the guy died.

Sirens split the air, and Minx knew he had to let go. If he killed Sepher, the cops might not be too happy with him. It took every ounce of self-restraint to not kill the bastard. Minx let go, and Sepher dropped to the floor. He was breathing, but he wasn't conscious.

The police rushed in seconds after Sunshine ran to Minx. He held onto her, praying the cops didn't shoot.

It took a few tense minutes for the cops to figure out exactly what had happened. By that time, Rawlins and the rest of his team, along with Mustang, Pid, and Midas, had shown up. A group of Navy officers, including Captain Ashford, were at his house, making sure the Honolulu police understood how much they wanted Sunshine's brother to suffer for what he'd done.

By the time the sun had risen midway up in the sky, the street out front of their house had cleared. Sunshine had showered and was sitting at the kitchen table along with Ashley and Becky. Jenna had just put Lila down for a nap and was fixing a sandwich for herself. The guys were helping him install a new bathroom door and clean up the bedroom.

"You know, we've been through a lot the last few weeks. We need time off," Vine said.

"We do," Legs said.

Minx chuckled. "I think taking a vacation sounds like a good idea."

Rawlins entered the room. "I heard from my connection in the police force that Sepher is on a plane to Louisiana. He's going to be on lockdown there for a good long time."

"He's such a little shit," Minx said.

"At least he's out of your hair." Vine finished with the door, testing it by swinging it shut. "The door looks good."

"Thank you all for helping out on this."

"Sure. Anytime you need us, we're here," Astro said.

"Astro, we're going to miss you when you get your own team," Vine said.

"Yeah, we'll miss you a lot," Wig said.

"I'll be around." Astro gave them all a hug before heading out to the kitchen with the women.

Minx followed the guys out to the main room. Sunshine was safe now. They didn't have to worry about Sepher anymore.

"Rawlins, the wedding is tomorrow. Will you be there?" Minx asked.

Rawlins flashed a smile. "I plan on it."

Sunshine moved to Rawlins and stuck out her hand. "Thank you. Your help means a lot."

Rawlins shrugged like it wasn't any big deal, and maybe to him, it wasn't, but it was to Minx. The man had helped save Sunshine.

"Anytime. I'm happy to help."

Sunshine shook Rawlins's hand then moved close to Minx. "Thank you all for helping."

Minx put his arm around his woman and pulled her close. "Yeah, you all are the best. This has been a difficult time, but thanks to you all, we're going to make it through."

Sunshine put her arm around his back and hugged him close. He kissed her cheek then turned to his friends. "We're here for you all, too."

"You've done so much for us," Vine said.

"Yes, thank you for everything," Robert added.

Minx couldn't have picked better friends. Everything had turned out great. It could have been much worse. Thank goodness they finished with their training when they did. He didn't want to think about what would have happened if they'd been delayed. Sepher would have had Sunshine.

The guys were tired and ready to leave. They said

goodbye to everyone, then he shut the door and pulled Sunshine in for a lingering kiss.

"You should get some sleep."

"Not sure that I can."

"How about I give you a blowjob to relax you, and we'll see if you can sleep."

Minx flashed her a smile and grabbed her hand as he headed toward the bedroom. "If you're offering, then I'm willing."

"Good. Because I'm going to need you recharged for tomorrow."

Minx took a quick shower, thinking that even with the blowjob, he would have a hard time falling asleep. He was wrong.

CHAPTER 26

The morning of their wedding, Sunshine woke in Minx's arms and wasn't surprised when he pulled her close and made love to her. Once they were up and showered, they had about twenty minutes before they had to leave.

"Are you ready?" Minx asked as she stepped out of the bedroom, her dress in a bag.

"Of course. I'm going to put my dress on there."

"You don't want to let me see first?"

"Heck no. You're going to see it when I step out from whatever is hiding me."

Minx flashed her a smile that made her knees weak. "I'm so glad you gave me a chance."

"Baby, you're my one and only."

"That's good because I feel the same way."

They drove over to the park, and Sunshine used the restroom with Becky and Ashley's help to get dressed. The dress wasn't much, but it was special because these women had helped her find it then altered it to fit her perfectly. She was happy with how she looked. No, it wasn't some white concoction with a long train, but it was exactly what she wanted. She didn't need extra because Ethan brought all the extra to the relationship. He would be a handful, but it came with a side of caring and love so deep she knew she would never want for love.

The music started, and they made their way outside, all three women blocking the guys' view of Sunshine until she was about twenty feet from where Ethan stood with the woman they'd hired to do the ceremony. They decided to keep the ceremony plain because neither one of them had strong ties to any church.

When her friends stepped to the side and Ethan saw her, his eyes lit up, taking in the pale blue dress she'd chosen for the wedding. She walked toward him, knowing she was walking toward her future.

Saying their vows was quick, and they both had tears in their eyes by the end of the service. When they kissed at the end, she knew she'd made the right choice. Ethan had brought love and wonder into her life. He'd completed her, and she knew based on the look in his eyes, she completed him.

The End

ABOUT THE AUTHOR

Julia Bright is the author of the contemporary military romance Dark Eagle series and is an Operation Alpha Author. Julia lives in the south where "bless your heart" is an insult and "shut up" shows love. Julia has been reading since they could open a book and has taken the passion for words and combined it with the love of travel to create stories full of passion and excitement. If you love a good book with a fantastic happily ever after, you'll enjoy a Julia Bright novel. For a dash of paranormal romance and urban fantasy, pick up a book from Julia's USA Today Bestselling JS Bright pen name

facebook.com/AuthorJuliaBright
amazon.com/Julia-Bright/e
bookbub.com/authors/julia-bright

OTHER BOOKS BY JULIA BRIGHT

Finding Home

Jenna's SEAL

Ashley's SEAL

Becky's SEAL

Sunshine's SEAL

Fighting for Home

A SEAL for Candace

A SEAL for Deb

A SEAL for Elise

A SEAL for Trixie

A SEAL for Raven

Special Forces: Operation Alpha

Saving Lorelei

Rescuing Amy

Saving Sloan

Seeking Justice

Justice for Amber

Searching for Keeley

Justice for Oswin

Safety for Eve

Dark Eagle Series

Survive The Fall

Live Past The Edge

Hold on Through the Pain

Endure the Darkness

Storm Corp Series

Determined

Standalone Romance

Acting The Part

All Business

Just One Taste

There are many more books in this fan fiction world than listed here, for an up-to-date list go to www.AcesPress.com

You can also visit our Amazon page at:
http://www.amazon.com/author/operationalpha

Special Forces: Operation Alpha World

Christie Adams: Charity's Heart
Denise Agnew: Dangerous to Hold
Shauna Allen: Awakening Aubrey
Linzi Baxter: Unlocking Dreams
Jennifer Becker: Hiding Catherine
Alice Bello: Shadowing Milly
Heather Blair: Rescue Me
Misha Blake: Flash
Anna Blakely: Rescuing Gracelynn
Julia Bright: Saving Lorelei
Cara Carnes: Protecting Mari
Kendra Mei Chailyn: Beast
Melissa Kay Clarke: Rescuing Annabeth
Samantha A. Cole: Handling Haven
Lorelei Confer: Protecting Sara
KaLyn Cooper: Spring Unveiled
Janie Crouch: Storm
Sarah Curtis: Securing the Odds

Jordan Dane: Redemption for Avery

Tarina Deaton: Found in the Lost

Aspen Drake, Intense

Riley Edwards: Protecting Olivia

PJ Fiala: Defending Sophie

Nicole Flockton: Protecting Maria

Hope Ford: Rescuing Karina

Alexa Gregory: Backdraft

Michele Gwynn: Rescuing Emma

Casey Hagen: Shielding Nebraska

Desiree Holt: Protecting Maddie

Kathy Ivan: Saving Sarah

Kris Jacen, Be With Me

Jesse Jacobson: Protecting Honor

Silver James: Rescue Moon

Becca Jameson: Saving Sofia

Kate Kinsley: Protecting Ava

Rayne Lewis: Justice for Mary

Heather Long: Securing Arizona

Margaret Madigan: Bang for the Buck

Ellie Masters: Sybil's Protector

Trish McCallan: Hero Under Fire

Rachel McNeely: The SEAL's Surprise Baby

KD Michaels: Saving Laura

Lynn Michaels: Rescuing Kyle

Olivia Michaels: Protecting Harper

Wren Michaels: The Fox & The Hound
Annie Miller: Securing Willow
Kat Mizera: Protecting Bobbi
Keira Montclair: Wolf and the Wild Scots
LeTeisha Newton: Protecting Butterfly
Angela Nicole: Protecting the Donna
MJ Nightingale: Protecting Beauty
Victoria Paige: Reclaiming Izabel
Anne L. Parks: Mason
Debra Parmley: Protecting Pippa
Danielle Pays: Defending Sarina
Lainey Reese: Protecting New York
KeKe Renée: Protecting Bria
TL Reeve and Michele Ryan: Extracting Mateo
Elena M. Reyes: Keeping Ava
Deanna L. Rowley: Saving Veronica
Angela Rush: Charlotte
Rose Smith: Saving Satin
Lynne St. James: SEAL's Spitfire
Dee Stewart: Conner
Harley Stone: Rescuing Mercy
Sarah Stone: Shielding Grace
Jen Talty: Burning Desire
Reina Torres, Rescuing Hi'ilani
Savvi V: Loving Lex
Megan Vernon: Protecting Us

LJ Vickery: Circus Comes to Town
Rachel Young: Because of Marissa
R. C. Wynne: Shadows Renewed

Delta Team Three Series

Lori Ryan: Nori's Delta
Becca Jameson: Destiny's Delta
Lynne St James, Gwen's Delta
Elle James: Ivy's Delta
Riley Edwards: Hope's Delta

Police and Fire: Operation Alpha World

Freya Barker: Burning for Autumn
B.P. Beth: Scott
Jane Blythe: Salvaging Marigold
Julia Bright, Justice for Amber
Anna Brooks, Guarding Georgia
KaLyn Cooper: Justice for Gwen
Aspen Drake: Sheltering Emma
Hadley Finn: Exton
Emily Gray: Shelter for Allegra
Alexa Gregory: Backdraft
Deanndra Hall: Shelter for Sharla
EM Hayes: Gambling for Ashleigh
India Kells: Shadow Killer
CM Steele: Guarding Hope

Reina Torres: Justice for Sloane
Aubree Valentine, Justice for Danielle
Maddie Wade: Finding English
Laine Vess: Justice for Lauren

Tarpley VFD Series

Silver James, Fighting for Elena
Deanndra Hall, Fighting for Carly
Haven Rose, Fighting for Calliope
MJ Nightingale, Fighting for Jemma
TL Reeve, Fighting for Brittney
Nicole Flockton, Fighting for Nadia

As you know, this book included at least one character from Susan Stoker's books. To check out more, see below.

SEAL Team Hawaii Series

Finding Elodie

Finding Lexie

Finding Kenna

Finding Monica (May 2022)

Finding Carly (Oct 2022)

Finding Ashlyn (Feb 2023)

Finding Jodelle (TBA)

Eagle Point Search & Rescue

Searching for Lilly (Mar 2022)

Searching for Elsie (Jun 2022)

Searching for Bristol (Nov 2022)

Searching for Caryn (TBA)

Searching for Finley (TBA)

Searching for Heather (TBA)

Searching for Khloe (TBA)

The Refuge Series

Deserving Alaska (Aug 2022)

Deserving Henley (Jan 2023)

Deserving Reese (TBA)

Deserving Cora (TBA)

Deserving Lara (TBA)

Deserving Maisy (TBA)

Deserving Ryleigh (TBA)

Delta Team Two Series

Shielding Gillian

Shielding Kinley

Shielding Aspen

Shielding Jayme (novella)

Shielding Riley

Shielding Devyn

Shielding Ember

Shielding Sierra

SEAL of Protection: Legacy Series

Securing Caite (FREE!)

Securing Brenae (novella)

Securing Sidney

Securing Piper

Securing Zoey

Securing Avery

Securing Kalee

Securing Jane

Delta Force Heroes Series

Rescuing Rayne (FREE!)

Rescuing Aimee (novella)

Rescuing Emily

Rescuing Harley

Marrying Emily (novella)

Rescuing Kassie

Rescuing Bryn

Rescuing Casey

Rescuing Sadie (novella)

Rescuing Wendy

Rescuing Mary

Rescuing Macie (novella)

Rescuing Annie

Badge of Honor: Texas Heroes Series

Justice for Mackenzie (FREE!)

Justice for Mickie

Justice for Corrie

Justice for Laine (novella)

Shelter for Elizabeth

Justice for Boone

Shelter for Adeline

Shelter for Sophie

Justice for Erin

Justice for Milena

Shelter for Blythe
Justice for Hope
Shelter for Quinn
Shelter for Koren
Shelter for Penelope

SEAL of Protection Series

Protecting Caroline (FREE!)
Protecting Alabama
Protecting Fiona
Marrying Caroline (novella)
Protecting Summer
Protecting Cheyenne
Protecting Jessyka
Protecting Julie (novella)
Protecting Melody
Protecting the Future
Protecting Kiera (novella)
Protecting Alabama's Kids (novella)
Protecting Dakota

New York Times, *USA Today* and *Wall Street Journal* Bestselling Author Susan Stoker has a heart as big as the state of Tennessee where she lives, but this all American girl has also spent the last fourteen years living in Missouri, California, Colorado, Indiana, and Texas. She's married to a retired Army man who now gets to follow *her* around the country.

www.stokeraces.com
www.AcesPress.com
susan@stokeraces.com

Made in the USA
Monee, IL
12 August 2022

11485187R00138